THE QUIET ROOM

Sian E. Jones

Grosvenor House
Publishing Limited

The right of Sian E. Jones to be identified as the author of this
work has been asserted in accordance with Section 78
of the Copyright, Designs and Patents Act 1988

This book is published by
Grosvenor House Publishing Ltd
Link House
140 The Broadway, Tolworth, Surrey, KT6 7HT.
www.grosvenorhousepublishing.co.uk

This book is a work of fiction. Any resemblance to
people or events, past or present, is purely coincidental.

A CIP record for this book
is available from the British Library

ISBN 978-1-83975-892-8

PART 1

Chapter 1

It was the symmetry of Celyn that pleased the eye. As she traipsed down her familiar path to prepare breakfast for the Demengels, Nancy considered which season showcased the house at its best. Today the wisteria hung in vivid lilac loops, framing the latticed windows which were "bugger difficult to clean" according to Cally Newby whose job it was to bring them to a shine.

Celyn had been employing the services of the natives of Landscove for generations. It was as familiar to Nancy as it was to the Demengel family. Her mother was the original Mrs Cooke, the cook. Nancy wondered idly which had come first, the name or the occupation.

As the cook, Nancy enjoyed the elevated status of living in one of the lodges on the estate after years of living in the annex of the main house. She had served her time living cheek by jowl with the other domestic staff and now cherished every nook and cranny of her compact cottage. Nancy had created an appealing space for herself to share with generations of border terriers, all named Wesley to avoid confusion. Her mother had optimistically embroidered, sown and knitted an extensive "bottom drawer" for Nancy, which now adorned every piece of furniture, softening the grey stones of the cottage walls and the flagged floor. Nancy had never been considered a great beauty. Her features were round and soft, and she had small brown eyes, which gave her the appearance of a kindly currant bun. She had managed to avoid wedlock and instead devoted herself to her love of all things pastry and fur. She seemed to be permanently enveloped in a cloud of flour; her made-for-pastry chunky hands either pummeling dough into submission or burying themselves in the hairy whorls of the current Wesley.

On this morning, the sun was already making a bold entrance and promised a searing heat by midday. Nancy thought about the day ahead and how she could organise her work, hoping to break the back of the day's menu before the midday sun turned the kitchen into a furnace. Over the past two years her ankles had begun to swell painfully in the heat, the skin pulled taut across her bones, like cloth pulled taut across a tapestry ring.

A faint splash and a plaintive cry caught her attention. Instinctively, Nancy strode to the pool. Many years before, the river had been banked and dammed to create a deep pool enjoyed by the Demengels and their visitors. It was deep and brackish and always, always icy. "Fresh and invigorating," they said. "Bleddy freezing more like," Nancy thought. They had even managed to fashion a diving board across the deepest part. It was a rite of passage for the Demengel brood to do a back flip into the depths.

Lara. Her long white cotton nightgown was coiling itself around her pale thin legs which appeared yellow under the surface of the pool. Lara, twin of Milla. Nancy briefly hesitated and wondered if there was an alternative to the inevitable course of action she was about to embark on. She hated the water and was no longer nimble. She looked around wildly for a stick to pass out to the flailing child. Lara was slipping beneath the surface and taking large gulps of air. There was nobody else around at this early hour to shout to for help. Resigned, Nancy scrambled down the grassy bank, barely noticing the rocks and stones assaulting her legs. She tried to get some purchase on the nightgown, but Lara slipped from her grasp. She went under the water again. "Oh shit, I'm going to have to go in," she thought, terrified. Trying to fight a rising tide of panic, Nancy clumsily flopped into the water. The icy water immediately enveloped her, and she gasped. Her limbs stiffened in the cold water making her feel leaden. She managed to grab a fistful of Lara's night gown and hauled her unceremoniously to the bank. Nancy lay back on the bank, trying to recover her breath. She was shaking violently, from cold and fear. Lara, lying beside her, began to laugh.

"Your face, Nancy! You all wet. Like a seal," she said, and kept laughing.

"I saw you, Nancy. I wanted to see you swim."

It suddenly dawned on Nancy that she had been duped. Again.

Nancy hovered between relief and fury.

"Look what you done to my poorly legs," Nancy pulled up her skirts to reveal some impressive grazes along her doughy calves and knees. Lara laughed harder.

"Right Miss. I am off to tell your mother and your father what mischief you have been up to today," already knowing she would do no such thing. The mistress could barely conceal her displeasure when she had occasion to look at Lara and Mr. Demengel had been given to "nerves" since his return from the Great War. Nancy felt it would serve no purpose except to re-ignite the fans of discontent when it came to matters about Lara.

Together, dripping wet, they made their way to the house. Lara tried to grasp Nancy's hand, but she was still too cross and pulled away from her. But by the time they reached the kitchen, Lara had managed to wheedle her way back into Nancy's affections.

"We had better get you a warm drink and something to eat, young Miss," Nancy said, trying to effect a gruff tone.

Nancy was starting to warm up; between the heat of the day and the range, which was ready, fired up for her day's tasks, she was thawing out. Sitting at the scrubbed table, Lara glugged down her drink and crammed bread into her mouth. Nancy thought it was little wonder Lara was excluded from dining with the rest of the Demengels. She ate as if she was starved and had been raised by wolves. As always, a gnawing anxiety clawed at Nancy's heart as she looked at the child. What would become of Lara? She was regarded with bewilderment and disdain by the entire household. There was no doubt she was an oddity for sure, thought Nancy. She was given to fits of violence and screaming and had ceased verbal communication with all but Nancy and animals. Milla was terrified of her temper and had long since abandoned any notion of twinship. She bore a scar down her left cheek; four scratch marks which served as a permanent reminder not to carry any tales to mother.

"Off with you now, Lara. This food won't make itself," Nancy said.

Lara came and leaned in to Nancy's side. It could not be described as an embrace. But it was the closest Lara came to physical contact. Nancy kissed the crown of her head. It was still damp and smelled brackish.

"Bye, Nancy. Come swim with me again."

Despite herself, she smiled wryly.

"Maybe, Lara, maybe."

Chapter 2

Nancy had never seen herself as particularly maternal. She was fond of her long line of Wesleys but felt she had dodged a bullet by not having children herself. She had barely glanced at the other Demengel brood, but Lara had foisted herself on Nancy as an infant.

Lara had been a cranky baby. Three staff had been drawn in to look after the twin girls. Milla was placid and slept peacefully whilst Lara's screams echoed around the chambers and corridors of Celyn.

"She won't be soothed," complained one wet nurse, an experienced woman who had tended Emmeline, Bertie and Theo with no such problems. "Not even for the Mistress," she observed. It was true. Lara stiffened in her mother's arms. In desperation, they asked if Nancy could prepare some sweet substance to pacify the infant. Nancy caramelised some sugar with the smallest drop of rum and took it up to the nursery herself. The wet nurse asked Nancy if she could hold Lara whilst she prepared to dip her little finger in the sticky pool to give to Lara. The child was rigid and fractious. Nancy sat in the large rocker as the baby was placed in her arms. Immediately, Lara stilled and nestled herself against the warmth of Nancy's bosom. The wet nurse swiveled her head in shock to see what Nancy had done.

"Well stone me," she said, as she looked at the scene before her.

A warmth flooded through Nancy as she gazed at the little scrap in her arms. She had felt something similar when she had first picked up the original Wesley. She pressed her nose to Lara's little head and drank in the sweet fragrance of her newness. Once she had settled, and the redness from her screaming had faded, Nancy could make out her features. The child was beautiful. Alabaster skin that would surely freckle in the sun, and dark blue eyes framed prettily by black lashes. A tiny nose and a crimson little mouth were all set in a perfect heart shaped face, crowned with a thatch of thick black hair. Under her right eye was a small dark birthmark, shaped almost like a star. It was the defining mark that distinguished her from Milla. That and her size. Milla was out-thriving Lara, smiling and gurgling contentedly, charming parents and caregivers alike. And already Lara was establishing herself as a problem.

It was only Nancy who could pacify her. And so it was that the call for cook to come to the nursery became a daily routine until Lara was old enough to navigate her own way to the kitchens.

"That child is feral," observed Cally Newby as she narrowly dodged Lara haring across the kitchen

"Her is proper cakey; half-baked her. Is no wonder she is Nancy's pet," Cally said to nobody in particular, chuckling at her own joke. Nancy felt a surge of anger and immediately jumped to Lara's defense.

"I will hear none of that talk in this kitchen," she said, and glowered at Cally who looked suitably chastened.

Lara made her way to seek succour with Nancy at every opportunity, a safe haven from the rigid expectations of being a Demengel.

By the age of six, she was already of deep concern to her parents. The twins were the youngest of the Demengel children. Their arrival was something of a surprise to everyone, as Charles Demengel had returned from the war forever changed. He was remote and edgy, and was treated by both his family and the household as an unpredictable loose cannon. He alternated between shouting rages and crying uncontrollably. He was largely confined to the drawing room maintaining close proximity to his whiskey decanter. Bertie and Theo were away at school in Launceston. There were high hopes for the girls to dazzle the fine families of Cornwall with their wit and pretty manners. Emmeline was already an emergent beauty with the trademark Demengel blue eyes and black hair. Milla was neat and graceful and a delight to the household. She had tried to engage Lara in her games, but she was too restless to settle to a sedate dolls tea party and had no interest in imaginative play. Milla was both fearful and fascinated by Lara in equal measure, her untamed mirror image. Lara was already beyond the control of her parents and the two governesses who had abruptly left, unable to manage her. Nancy provided warmth, but even she had little in the way of control over her behaviour. It was her speed and relentless energy that was so wearing. And the impulsivity - it was impossible to predict what might take her fancy to do in any given moment. Random, scandalous and without even a passing nod for any consequences, Lara did whatever she pleased. Punishment had not a jot of impact on her. It was impossible to gauge whether she had any emotional attachment to either her parents or to her other siblings. She had the scantest regard for Milla who she considered boring and silly. Lara's gaze was intense, but it was impossible to discern if she was penetrating your very soul or not seeing you at all.

A tutor for the twins was recruited from Porthmon. Miss Vernon had been briefed on the challenges posed by Lara and had been determined to tame the excesses of her behaviour. She had a good reputation and was known for her no-nonsense approach with her charges. Miss Vernon was reedish; tall, and thin, and seemed to Lara to be badly drawn with all straight edges. She detested her on sight. She also had a vinegary smell which seemed to compound the air of bitterness that wafted around her.

Miss Vernon suggested that Lara was "backward in her learning" and the tutor soon became more keeper than tutor. She quickly became exasperated with her and took to physical control, grabbing her spindly arms and thin wrists, her cruelty escalating daily as her frustration grew. Lara managed to squirm her way out of her grasp to escape either outdoors or to the sanctuary of the kitchen and to the comfort of Nancy. One day she managed to grab Lara by the shoulders and tried to tie her into a chair with a thin piece of rope. She was determined to subdue her charge and force her into submission and was unwilling to admit defeat over one so small. So violently did Lara struggle to free herself, she slid down the chair. The rope looped around her neck. The more she struggled, the tighter the rope entangled itself until eventually she was being strangled. With her breath beginning to leave her, she kicked

Miss Vernon with as much ferocity as she could. Lara's foot caught her in her groin, causing Miss Vernon to let out a shriek of pain which alerted Cally Newby, who happened to be passing with a mop and bucket. Cally rushed into the room. She shouted for help as she struggled to untie Lara who had a livid rope mark around her neck.

"Oh, what have you done, Miss?" she said to Miss Vernon, who had visibly paled. She felt sick at what would happen now. She frantically tried and failed to concoct a story to try and explain why she had tied Lara in a chair. With a sick, heavy realisation that she could have killed the child, Miss Vernon accepted her dismissal and walked stiffly away from Celyn Lodge. If she had taken a backward glance, she would have seen Lara Demengel watching her leave, with a small, satisfied smile. Lara never went to the classroom again.

Chapter 3

Charles and Loveday Demengel were at a loss as how to manage her. Charles abdicated all responsibility for her, fearing she bore the same curse as his older sister Morwenna. She had been something of a wild card. She had been older than him by ten years and his memories of her were vague. She was never spoken of again after she drowned herself in the millpond in Landscove when she disgraced herself with a village farmhand. Charles had been six at the time. It was as if Morwenna had never existed and her footprints in Celyn scrubbed from its collective memory.

Dr Franklin had served the family for eighteen years. He prescribed a cocktail of tinctures which only served to increase Lara's restlessness, and did not have the sedating effect they had desired. He suggested sending her away to an institution where she could be cared for properly. Dr Franklin also suggested physical chastisement. He suggested everything bar exorcism, none of it making any difference to the increasingly hard to tolerate conduct. Loveday despaired at her daughter and worried about her potential to tarnish the reputation of the family in Landscove and beyond. Emmeline was concerned Lara could seriously damage her chances of securing a husband from a desirable family.

One autumn day, a solution began to reveal itself to Loveday as she once again went looking for Lara. Milla was inconsolable after Lara had beheaded Daisy Mae, her beloved doll. Poor Milla, she thought. It's not fair on her. It's not fair on any of us. She felt the usual bitter anger and resentment for Lara. Why couldn't she just be normal, like other children? She wondered what she could have done to deserve such a curse on her life; it was a blight, a punishment, she thought, as she descended into the melee of the kitchen hoping to find her. A wave of heat greeted her, and the warm smell of apricots caused her mouth to water. The kitchen was large and welcoming. Loveday thought she could understand why her daughter was drawn to the cheery chatter of the women gossiping while they were busy chopping, rolling, and kneading. Nancy was creating scallop shapes into the crust of a pie. Lara was cutting out some shapes with a small sheet of pastry. Loveday felt a stab of jealousy that her daughter chose a lowly cook to bestow her affection upon instead of her own mother. She who had laboured to bring her into the world. Lara barely acknowledged her mother. She regarded her coolly and carefully plunged her cutter through to the cool marble table beneath her.

It didn't take much persuasion for Charles to agree Loveday's plan.

Nancy was summoned to the drawing room the next morning. Anxiety gnawed at her insides. She had barely set foot in the drawing room but felt clumsy and unwieldly amongst the finery of the furnishings. She felt at home in the kitchen, queen of her castle. She was wary of Master Demengel and had made a successful career of avoiding him since she had witnessed him fighting an invisible assailant in the early dawn light one morning, a year after the war had ended. She declined his offer of a seat. Without preamble, Charles, laid out his proposal.

He reminded Nancy how privileged she was, occupying an estate cottage. Nancy's heart sank at this reminder that she was beholden to the family. Her stomach lurched and her hands became trembled and became sweaty. Her eye was caught by a large blackbird on the lawn and in that moment, she envied it it's freedom.

Charles spoke to her as if he were barking orders at one of his infantry men.

In return for her continued tenure of the cottage, they required Nancy to become Lara's full-time custodian. She would, of course be relieved of her duties in the kitchen and would receive a generous stipend for her efforts. Nancy would guard Lara and keep her safely tucked away from the family home unless instructed otherwise. She would be well provided for and supplies would be delivered to the cottage. Under no circumstances was Lara to go into Landscove. She was to be, as far as possible, hidden from view. She was permitted to use the pool when there were no visitors and down to the small cove that could only be accessed through the wooded glades of Celyn.

Nancy soon realised this was not a proposal but a fait accompli. She barely had time to hang up her apron before taking Lara to her new home in the wooded area obscured from Celyn where Nancy's cottage nestled surrounded by trees. She was eight years old.

Chapter 4

If Lara missed her family, or Celyn, she showed no outward signs of it. Initially, Nancy felt miffed that Miss Grainger from the village had usurped her, but she was much cheered by reports from Cally that her pastry was dense and her souffle was as flat as skinny Patsy Glover's breasts. She slowly acknowledged that the daily grind had been taking its toll on her health. She was breathless at times and though she would never say anything, had some twinges in the left side of her chest.

Nancy and Lara effortlessly developed their own rhythm. Nancy still rose early but often found Lara already up, already laying out flour, butter and sugar ready to bake. Nancy chuntered all day; it seemed to soothe Lara, who was altogether calmer and sometimes hummed little tunes to herself. Wesley would wait in keen expectation of scraps from his new devoted best friend to whom he was now welded. Together they tried out new recipes with Lara always adding her own little flourish, a W for Wesley or a pastry leaf on a pie. She would gravitate towards Nancy every evening to lean in to her side, the only one in her world to be permitted physical contact. It was the happiest and most settled Lara had ever been.

"Go on with you to bed," Nancy would say. Lara went without argument; she loved the sturdy wooden bed and the pretty patchwork quilt made by Nancy's mother. She liked the picture of Jesus holding his bleeding heart and the yellow jug on the chest that always had wild flowers in it. Nancy would plant a kiss on her forehead before heading to bed herself. She was never far behind her - the child was exhausting! Nancy had never imagined the paradox of joy and anxiety a child could bring.

Cally Newby called round with the hope of eliciting some litany of complaint from Nancy about her charge to pass on to the below stairs gossip mill.

"Her is fierce protective," bemoaned Cally to Miss Grainger.

"She practically shoved me over the threshold when I said her was simple. She will be the death of poor Nancy, mark my words," she stated with conviction. "They should send her away." Miss Grainger had never met Lara and listened with an appalled fascination as Cally recounted some tales of the wild Demengel child.

Celyn was built on a headland on the southern tip of Cornwall; its granite walls standing brave against the savage winds and storms for centuries. A well-worn sandy path had been forged in the wild grasses by generations of Demengels and the Rosewarne dynasty before them, down to a narrow cove. It was fringed by a bracelet of rocks that created an illusion of a pool, azure blue in the summer and an angry, gunmetal grey in the winter.

"Come on lazy legs," Nancy called to Lara and she would laugh, as her legs were far from lazy.

"You are lazy legs," Lara laughed. Her speech was fast, with a paucity of vocabulary, but she had no difficulty in making herself understood.

Wesley and Lara would race through the grove towards the beach while Nancy ambled behind at her own pace. Nancy thought they probably did 20 miles to her two, but Lara had so much energy to expend. Lara and Wesley were often already playing in the waves by the time Nancy had negotiated the path to the shoreline.

"Come in Nancy! It fun,"

"Don't go out too far, Lara!" Nancy would shout, but her admonishment fell on deaf ears. Lara and Wesley were already far from reach. Nancy soon learned that the sea was the only thing Lara seemed to respect. She was a fierce little swimmer but knew her limits and understood the twists and turns of the tide. She remembered with wry amusement the morning she had risked life and limb to rescue her from the pool; she was never in any danger, and she knew it.

In the summer, her pale skin turned a deep caramel colour that Loveday Demengel would have winced at. There was no doubt she was a beautiful child – and her sapphire blue eyes were such a stark contrast to her long dark hair. Her little upturned nose had seemingly strategically placed freckles as if they had been drawn on to be aesthetically pleasing. And of course, the little star shaped birthmark. Like a final flourish on a beautiful painting.

Nancy had tried to "learn Lara some words" but Lara had no interest, and with no small relief as Nancy had little to offer in that regard, so they abandoned any pretense of structured education.

But Lara could soon identify every herb in Nancy's little "kitchen garden" and how to use it to flavour her cooking. She watched Nancy intently as she took a cup of this, a handful of that, a dash of something else.

It wasn't the only thing Lara noticed. She said nothing but she traced with her finger a thin blue line that had developed above Nancy's top lip. It was as if someone had drawn a horizontal line with ink that followed the curve of her lip. She also noticed her hands were puffy, like a bear's paw and her ankles had lost their form with her calves and ankles seemingly fused together, no longer distinguishable as separate body parts.

Loveday's visits diminished over time. She had nurtured a vain hope that Lara would change, would perhaps miss her and would want to come home, subdued and contrite. She thought perhaps she would be repentant and tire of Nancy and her lowly living. That she might miss Milla and her well-appointed bedroom. Conversely, Lara seemed happier than ever before. Although more tanned than she should be, and resembling a village child, she had to concede she was thriving. Nancy had tried to ensure Lara looked respectable for these maternal visits and tried to wrestle her into her Sunday best clothes. Although why she still had Sunday best clothes was anyone's guess, as Loveday had told Nancy that Lara must not, under any circumstances, attend church.

St Bede's Parish Church of Landscove was no place for the likes of Lara. The Demengels had their own pew and were much lauded by the villagers as a potential source of employment and to gawp at Emmeline and latterly Milla with their fine clothes and grand manners. Lara balked about dressing up for her mother and would pull her hair out of the plaits Nancy had painstakingly fashioned and tied with ribbons. She would run into the garden and roll around on the dampened grass and mud. Loveday could barely conceal her distaste for this child who caused her so much pain. They had concocted a web of lies around what had become of Lara. She was incandescent with rage when Lara ignored her or when she saw her looking like a wild gypsy child. Why, oh why, could she not be more like Milla? She sobbed hot, racking tears when she had seen Lara laugh at something Nancy had said and heard her say something back. She had not heard her own daughter's voice in two years. As far as she was aware, neither had anyone else. Nancy was wary of telling Loveday that Lara still spoke to her, often and loudly, fearing the pain this would cause her. The family had created a narrative that Lara had gone to stay with Loveday's sister in Devon. The enquiries eventually abated, and it was as if Milla had never had a twin.

Chapter 5

Nancy was finding it increasingly difficult to move about. She didn't say anything but had started to make groaning noises when she had to heave herself up from a chair or walk any distance. She said to Cally she felt like she had "an all over toothache". She was short of breath; her body felt leaden as if she were walking through treacle. The blue line above her lip was more pronounced now. She had less of a leash on Lara these days, especially since Lara and Nancy had managed to acquire a horse which was now a firm fixture at the cottage.

"Get this horse out of my kitchen Lara," Nancy would say, simultaneously blowing up his nostrils and feeding him sweet apples across the stable door in the back kitchen. Lara laughed.

" I go for ride now. On Solomon."

Lara rode like she swam; she was nimble and adept. The flimsy control Nancy had over her was gone. Lara rode when and where she pleased. Nancy had no idea where she was going. Lara would return, energised and flushed with exertion. Nancy fretted over whether she should tell the Demengels, but she wasn't convinced they would care, unless it adversely affected them or caused them embarrassment. Cally still visited to keep Nancy up to date with the gossip. She told Nancy it was as if Lara had disappeared into the annals of time. Theo and Bertie were busy establishing themselves in London, Emmeline was "out" in society and Milla was genteel, kind and studious. Cally urged Nancy to give up the girl - "she be killing you", but Nancy shuddered to think what would become of Lara without her. She had no choice but to carry on. Besides, she loved the girl. She had never wanted marriage and definitely not children, thinking she was not "the type". But she would move heaven and earth for Lara. She fretted over her constantly.

It was the end of October, and the summer was definitely over. The heat had gone out of the sun and the trees were starting their annual moult. Nancy woke up with a start. She felt a crushing pain in her chest. Roundly ignoring it, she got up.

"Lara," she called out, but she was too late. Nancy checked Wesley's bed - it was cool, so they must have been gone a while. She checked the field - the horse was gone too.

"That child will be the death of me," she said aloud.

This had happened so often so now that Nancy felt mildly irritated but was not overly concerned. She set the pot on the stove for tea and went to get dressed. "I should wash," she thought, but she felt exhausted. Feeling the cold in her bones, she pulled her warmest cardigan about her. She sat at the table and drank the tea, sweetened with honey the way she liked it. She buttered herself a scone - she did not bother with a plate - Wesley will polish off the crumbs, she decided. Nancy could not recall a time that she had missed her daily ablutions; "cleanliness is dreckly next to Godliness," her mother used to say. Nancy looked at her little kitchen. She smoothed her hand over the old mahogany table, reveling in its solidity. She used it now to lever herself up. Again, she felt pressure in her chest and hung over the table until it ebbed away. She had never been to a doctor in her life, but she thought she ought to see if Dr Franklin would give her the once over, although she did not like him one bit since he had drugged Lara and mentioned "putting her away".

Nancy would have left Lara to it, but Loveday Demengel was due to visit after church. The church bells of St. Bede's chimed across from Landscove village as they always had.

Heavily, Nancy lumbered in the direction of the grove to pick up the path to the beach. She looked over to Celyn. You could only see a glimpse of one turret from her cottage. Nancy had a sudden yearning to see Celyn in all its glory; to drink in its perfect symmetry in the Autumn glow. Occasionally she had missed the chaos and bustle of the kitchen and the friendship of her colleagues. She remembered fondly her own, albeit brief childhood playing in the grounds whilst her Mother sweated over the same range she had for years. She felt as much a part of the fabric of Celyn as the Demengels.

Nancy eventually came to the clearing. The salty breeze momentarily took her breath away and her eyes smarted. She fished out her little handkerchief from her cardigan pocket and held it against her eyes. She traced over the initials NC her mother had so lovingly stitched what felt like a lifetime ago. "The only delicate thing about me," mused Nancy as she returned the silky square to her pocket.

Solomon was chewing some coarse grass where the path met the beach. He paused momentarily to glance at Nancy before returning to graze. Wesley was lying faithfully in wait. She scoured the beach for Lara. Nancy could not fathom what she was looking at as her brain struggled to comprehend the scene unfolding before her. She felt violently ill, and her legs foundered beneath her. Lara was vigorously bucking back and forth over a prostate gentleman. Her face flushed with exertion, her expression unreadable. It was impossible to discern either pleasure or revulsion. The passive recipient of her energies had his trousers bunched by his ankles. Nancy was struck by how ridiculously thin and pale his legs looked. She was frozen. She could not shout out and her body was incapable of movement. Her eyes were still blurry and smarting from wiping them. Who was this? Did she know him? She did not recognize him, but as the pain gripped her chest and she fell to the ground, she noticed the boots. Gentleman's boots. Polished to a shine. And then there was darkness.

Chapter 6

Lara was alerted to Nancy's slumped body by Wesley's relentless barking. Jumping up in alarm, she ran over and began to shake Nancy as if to awaken her. She let out a primitive howl like a wild animal. The gentleman, who only moments before had been lying oblivious to all but his own pending nirvana, quickly took in the scene. Scrambling to pull up his breeches, he felt a wave of fear flood through him. He looked around furtively before heading off over the rocks to the less worn path towards Landscove. Lara had seen enough dead animals in her time to know Nancy was dead. The warmth was starting to leave her felled body. Lara felt a heaviness in her soul she had never felt before. She lay next to Nancy, willing her not to be dead. Night fell and still Lara and Wesley kept vigil beside her.

That was how they were found the next morning. Solomon had returned up the path to Celyn and was grazing on the formal front lawn of the house. Loveday had breathed a sigh of relief the day before, that neither Lara nor Nancy had been home when she called as planned after church. She had the beginnings of "one of her heads" and wanted to lie down. It was young Joff, the junior gardener who spotted him and called Mr. Hargreaves. Joff was terrified around horses and had no mind to approach the beast. Hargreaves recognized

Solomon. Putting a makeshift lead about the horse's neck, he led him to Nancy's cottage to return him to his rightful owner and get him off his precious lawn. He knocked at Nancy's door. He knocked again and then peered through the window. There was no sign of its occupants. Pushing the door open, he called out for Miss Nancy. All was as it had been left the previous morning.

Finding it a little odd that both Nancy and the child should be out so early, he put the horse in the paddock and pootled up to the house. He was curious more than concerned, and thought he would see If the Cally girl knew anything. Cally reported she had not seen her for a while.

"When do I have time to go gallivanting round the estate?" she asked. "Got a husband as well as this lot to clean up after." She thought old Hargreaves had an easy ride, fannying about pulling up a few weeds and deadheading roses.

"I will wander over this afternoon," she said, the thought of a gossip and a bit of cake cheering her.

It was not until the late afternoon that the alarm was finally raised, and a search party started. Cally called to the empty cottage and had run back to Celyn "with a sense of impending doom", she later recounted to anyone who would listen. It was Theo who made the unfortunate discovery. Nancy was stone dead and mottled purple by this time and Lara was lying still and seemingly asleep besides her. Even Wesley was motionless, only looking up briefly at Theo before returning to his position draped around Lara's neck like a scarf. For one dreadful moment, Theo thought it was Milla lying there, as if dead. But then he remembered he had just seen her at lunch time, picking fastidiously at her food and asking mother about a new dress. Relief flooded through him as he realised it was Lara, and to double check, scanned her face for her birthmark. Simultaneously he worried what Nancy's death would now mean for the family. She could not return to Celyn. She was feral. He had heard the rumors around Landscove of a mystery girl who seemed to provide something of a rite of passage to the young men of the village who wanted to be unburdened of their virginity. The skill with which she rode her horse had led them to the conclusion she was from one of the Romany tribes that lived in the far-flung moorlands. According to the gossip mill, she put up no argument and kept on returning for more so she must like it. Young Archie Blaine had blanched one Sunday morning when he saw Milla Demengel in one of "them pews for the posh folk" in church. He recalled with some shame his own dalliance with the odd girl who silently tolerated his clumsy fumblings. With some relief he saw it was not the same girl, just a close resemblance, as Milla sat prettily, flanked by her mother and brothers. Theo flushed puce when he thought of it as he was filled with disgust and shame for this repugnant girl who happened to be his sister. His shouts bought the search party to his aid.

Lara was parceled up and taken to Nancy's cottage where she was laid in a makeshift bed in front of a fire that had been hastily lit. Dr Franklin was summoned and said she was to be kept warm and pronounced she would in all probability be much the same after some rest and tender loving care. The only person capable of the tender and loving part of that request was newly dead, thought Loveday as she looked at her daughter with the realisation that she was now left to find a new solution to the problem of Lara. It would have been easier if Lara had not survived her night exposed to the elements she thought and tried to banish the unwelcome thought from her mind. Dr Franklin reassured Loveday that the matter was in hand, but his plan would take a few days to organize. "Trust me dear," he had said, patting her arm tenderly.

Cally Newby was appointed to take temporary custody of Lara until Dr Franklin's more permanent solution could be set in place. Ted was not best pleased, but they both knew they were powerless to object; they needed their job. And besides, they had been promised a bonus payment for their trouble. She was not overly delighted with the task and thought to herself she would never again complain about polishing up the silver. Had she known what was ahead, she would have simply refused the role.

In the early hours of the morning, Cally was woken by Lara screaming. Kicking off her bedclothes in irritation and trepidation, she went to see what was wrong. Lara was sat up in bed, sweating profusely and holding her stomach. When Cally approached, Lara took a wild swing at her, catching her painfully on the chin. The screaming came intermittently and Cally was at a complete loss as to what to do and she was terrified. She woke Ted who had been sleeping soundly, as usual, she thought with resentment. She sent him to summon someone from Celyn. "She needs the doctor," she said.

There was a weak light by the time Dr Franklin arrived. Taking one look at Lara, he ordered Ted to bring Tabitha Hollis from the village. He ordered Cally to prepare hot water and clean linens. Lara was oddly silent between contractions. Pushing her head into her chest as she bore down, she made a low baying sound. The fine capillaries in her face strained with exertion as she laboured. She struggled up and got on to all fours, rocking back and forwards. By the time Tabitha arrived, the baby's head was crowning. She surmised quickly that this was no ordinary birth; Dr Franklin would never have allowed such an unseemly birthing position. This was like something primitive, foreign.

"I will explain all afterwards," Dr Franklin said to Tabitha. "Right now, our job is to get this bastard out."

Finally, the baby slipped out. Tiny and blue, the silence was deafening. Tabitha cut the cord and she and Dr Franklin regarded each other, each trying to weigh up what to do. Dr Franklin had no intention of trying to resurrect the thing. This would destroy Loveday. He couldn't bear to see her beautiful features etched with the pain and disgrace this baby would cause. Lara was slumped back into the pillow now. Hearing nothing, she struggled to sit up. She looked from Tabitha to Dr Franklin to the tiny, lifeless baby lying between her legs. She scooped the flaccid bundle up and held it tightly to her chest. Picking up an edge of the sheet, she started to rub the baby's back with a firm hand.

"Please," Lara said, nobody knew to who. Breaking the silence, the baby gave a strangled cry. A smile crept up Lara's face as she looked at her baby with a look Tabitha would never forget. It was a mother's love. Lara stroked the baby's face and leant down and kissed the downy head. She inhaled deeply and drank in the smell of blood and new life. She held the baby close and could not tear her eyes away from this vision of beauty.

A girl. Jet black hair. Darkest of blue eyes. A faint impression of a red mottled butterfly across the bridge of her nose. Perfect lips, deep red, with a cupid bow. Ears like the intricate whorls of a flower. As Lara was studying her, Tabitha moved in to extricate her from her arms. Lara clamped her arms more tightly around the baby and violently shook her head.

"I need to look her over," Tabitha tried to explain. She looked helplessly at Dr Franklin who said he would deal with it. His efforts left him hunched in pain after Lara delivered a swift, well aimed kick. Tabitha leant down to help him up. Smarting and humiliated, he brushed her off. Cally had been sent to fetch Loveday. It was at this moment she came in. Taking in the scene, the devastated bedclothes, her daughter looking weak and fragile and holding one of the smallest babies she had ever seen, Loveday knew what unadulterated hatred felt like. Lara clung even more fiercely to the baby and glowered at her mother. It soon became clear that Lara would not hand the baby over without a struggle. They retreated to the kitchen and closed the door to discuss what was to be done. Left alone with her baby, Lara instinctively put the little girl to her breast to be fed.

Chapter 7

For the next 6 hours, Lara happily lay feeding and gazing at the child. She tolerated the presence of Cally as she brought in tea and food but refused to get up and be washed or allow clean sheets to be laid on the bed. So, it was in this bloodied bed that she was when Dr Franklin returned with a glass syringe and four capable looking men. She fought as much as she could but was no match for the sedatives now coursing through her bloodstream. Tabitha swooped in and bundled up the child from Lara's failing grip.

And so it was that on October 30th, 1937, 16-year-old Lara Demerge made her entrance into Wellswood Manor Hospital crudely strapped down to a trolley.

Meanwhile, Nancy had been laid to rest next to her mother and father in St. Bede's. The Demengels occupied the family pew, and the rest of the church was packed with house staff and villagers. The newish vicar, Rev. Donald Pinkerton conducted the service. When they said newish, he had been there for five years already but was still considered an outsider from Devon. Cally thought his name was apt as today he was indeed very pink and seemed nervous. He kept clearing his throat and there was a slight tremor to his hands. He was an unfortunate looking man, in his early 30's with a prematurely receding hairline and lips like livid offal, overly bloodied and slack. He had an insipid, uninspiring handshake that left one feeling damp and in need of a handwash. His sermons were bland and lacking in the gravitas of his predecessor. But Cally noticed an oddity when he stepped out from behind the lectern. His boots. Incongruously highly polished. Gentleman's boots.

PART 2

Wellswood Manor Hospital for the mentally subnormal 1975

Shelley Merrigan followed the directions to Cherry Ward where she was to have her medical examination before she was deemed fit to start working on the wards. She was greeted by Doctor Winstanley who extinguished a cigarette when Shelley entered the room and waved the smoke away pointlessly. Her accent was unfamiliar; she was from Canada which seemed glamorous to Shelley who had only left County Wicklow for the first time 48 hours before. The doctor had a no-nonsense attitude and no patience for small talk.

"You will gather by the noise you are in a madhouse," Dr Winstanley said. Shelley was not prepared for the noise despite her Ma saying, "Sure you are going from one madhouse to another." The noises were hard to describe; there was screaming, crying, and groaning but also unfamiliar noises she hadn't heard before but akin to a barnyard. It was true she had a large family back home in Wicklow where just two days before she had left her Mammy choking on big dry sobs as she got on the bus. Even her Da's eyes were shiny as he said, "Will you shush now Patti, you are making a common show of us all." But Shelley had been desperate to leave home and try to forget Connor O'Hare who had bust her heart open.

The other assault on her senses was the smell. "The smell of humanity in all its glory," Dr Winstanley said. Shelley couldn't adequately describe the smell in her first letter to Mammy, so wrote succinctly, "it stinks of shit".

Dr Winstanley did a few perfunctory checks on Shelley. "You are overweight - ideally you should have dropped a few pounds before we got you here. You will need to shift those before you start your training. You will need to run past the sweetshop."

Shelley felt her face burn with shame as she remembered overhearing her friend's Da saying "Jeez, she's built like a brick shit house," and that was after a week of eating nothing but grapefruit and boiled eggs in readiness for the school dance. There was no escaping it. She was a big girl, but strong and hardy. The doctor signed her off as fit and wished Shelley luck as she gave her directions.

"Next stop is the needle room to get measured for your uniform - down the corridor next to the laundry room." Shelley made her way down the corridor. She shrunk into the wall to make way for a large metal trolley which housed the dirty pans from lunch to be returned to the catering quarters. On the side of the trolley in what looked like paint was the name "David". The man pushing it was grimacing and sweating with the effort." Thanks Nurse," he said. Shelley turned the word Nurse over in her head. She didn't know the first thing about being a nurse; introductory block started tomorrow. She would not be a real nurse for three years – for now she was Student Nurse Merrigan. Three whole years in this strange place after which she would be an RNMS, Registered Nurse for the Mentally

Subnormal. She already longed for home, for Wicklow, even for her brothers and the mangey dog. She fought back hot tears as she found the needle room.

Not unkindly, Mrs Stewart visually measured Shelley. "Hmmm, you're a big girl. I might have some adjustments to make." Shelley was beginning to feel circus large, but in time she was handed a black trunk. The contents within were six blue and white checked dresses, two navy cardigans. a white belt to denote her role as Student Nurse - first year, and a blue gabardine coat with a shiny scarlet lining. There were also six paper hats which Mrs. Stewart had expertly shown her how to fold. Her name was written into all the items. Student Nurse Merrigan. She was told to return the trunk each week to the laundry to ensure she had a clean uniform daily.

The next stop was to find her way to the nurse's residence to find her home for the next three years. Bawtree House had six floors of cell type rooms. Each floor had two toilets and a bath. There was a small kitchen on every other floor. Shelley hesitated as she put her key in the lock. She wondered what she had done. She had been so desperate to leave Wicklow, and Cornwall had looked so beautiful, not unlike home, but with no sign of Connor Bastard O'Hare. But now she longed for the warm embrace of home. She stepped into the room and her spirit broke. Across the length of the room was a narrow single bed with a candlewick blanket. She was not confident it could contain her whole body. The pillow was as thin as a cracker and had dark brown patches, spread out like continents on an atlas. Dribble, she thought grimly. A small wardrobe and a three-drawer chest completed the room. There was a small sink in the corner with a yellow stain like a teardrop from the hot tap. The curtains were a sun-bleached faded orange, hanging loosely from a plastic rail. She slumped onto the bed and didn't even try and stem the flow of tears.

Chapter 8

Six weeks later, with Introductory block completed, Shelley went along to the allocations board to see where she would be doing her first placement. The wards were called villas and were spread across the hospital. The main administration block was an imposing building at the front of the hospital. Wellswood Manor Hospital had been built in 1870 and had housed the feeble minded of Cornwall for over a hundred years. The small town of Mallock had wrapped itself around the hospital with houses providing accommodation for "live out" staff; usually qualified or married with a family. The hospital was the main source of industry for Mallock. Wellswood had eighteen wards for the mentally subnormal, including two "lock up wards" - one male, one female. All the villas were named after trees and the grounds were well kept and expansive. The older staff and the patients had some difficulty trying to adopt the more favoured term of "mentally handicapped". The wards were separated into high- and low-grade wards. The patients would often hurl the overused insult of "you bleddy low grade", to each other. Aside from the lock up wards, the patients were free to roam about within the grounds. Indeed, many had jobs to go to within the hospital: in the laundry, on the farm, in the kitchens, the needle rooms and the gardens. There was also a small industrial unit which had packing and sorting jobs from local businesses. A few trustees were also permitted to work in the stores, sorting out the supplies for each ward. A tea shop, run by volunteers from the League of Friends, provided a social hub for the patients and a weekly dance, which was held on a Friday at lunchtime in the recreation hall, provided another chance to meet. It was like a small town in its own right and there was little reason to leave the perimeter walls. The strict segregation of men and women had tentatively been done away with; the staff no longer adopting a strict policing role with regards to relationships. Some of the women would exchange sexual favours for a few smokes and it was not unusual to stumble across those engaged in this trading of favours in the quieter areas of the hospital. Shelley was advised to turn a blind eye in these circumstances. Tobacco was currency and if you had smokes to trade, you were rich.

Student Nurse Merrigan. She found her name on the board and saw that her first placement was to be on Cypress Villa. It would be three months until her next school block. She tried to recall everything she had learned over the last six weeks. All the villas were named after trees. Cypress was one of the far-flung villas near the perimeter back gate which was a shortcut to Mallock and the nearest Chinese takeaway. It was about a four-minute walk from Bawtree House. Her shift started at 7am. On her first morning, she walked down the narrow path towards the villa, trying to summon a confidence she did not feel and to quell the rising tide of anxiety. She pushed open the double doors and there it was. That smell. That noise. Low moans, crying and shouting. Standing stock-still outside the office was a woman of indeterminate age. From her facial features, she could have been anywhere from twenty-five to eighty, her skin bore neither blemish nor line, except for a small mark beneath her right eye. She wore a thin nightdress that offered no protection from the chill of the morning. Her feet were bare and had a blue tinge, probably from the cold, Shelley assumed. Her hair was raven black with a smattering of grey and hung from a middle parting in long, straight swathes. Her stillness chilled Shelley. "Good morning," Shelley said. The older woman did not reply. Shelly was not sure if the woman was blind. Or maybe deaf? She looked at Shelley blankly.

"I am Nurse Merrigan," she ventured. The woman's long nightdress lent a further ethereal quality to the silence encircling them. Shelley was aware of the redness creeping up her own neck and could hear her own breathing. She suddenly felt a prickle of fear as she realised she had no script for this scenario; feeling as unsure as she might when meeting a strange dog and not knowing whether its silence was malevolent or not. Suddenly, the welcome sight of Sister Berry appeared.

"Well, come in - you have to report to me for duty each morning in the office. It is hand over time." Shooing the woman away she said. "Off you go Lara - you know I don't like you hanging around the office at hand over. And put on some slippers and a cardigan for goodness' sake. You will catch your death." Wordlessly, Lara drifted away.

After hand over, which appeared to Shelley to be no more than a ceremonial passing of a large bunch of keys from the night nurse who also said, "Henty has been playing up," it was time for duties to begin.

Shelley made up the staff number to four. This was apparently something of a luxury in a ward of twenty-eight women.

"You are supernumerary," Shelley was told, but by 9am she knew this to not be true.

"You can feed the babies," Sister Berry directed. The other tables had been laid for breakfast by the night staff. Each table was covered with a blue checked tablecloth, apart from the baby's table. There were knives, forks and spoons and blue plastic cups and saucers. There was a large teapot on two tables. These were for the "high grades", who were capable of pouring their own tea. The tea was already made with milk and sugar, so everyone had the same.

The "Babies" were four patients who were unable to feed themselves. Shelley had spooned four mouthfuls of porridge into one woman whose arms seemed to be in perpetual motion and who clamped on the spoon so hard it was difficult to pull it out, when she heard a loud cry. One of the ladies had fallen to the ground and was having a seizure. She wore some kind of helmet, plastic, lined with foam. The chinstrap left an indent under the jaw due to it being fastened so securely. "A frequent fitter," Sister Berry explained later.

"That's a grand mal seizure. The noise you heard was the Aura. That's the tonic phase and then there is the clonic phase. The thrashing about." Shelley had learnt about it in block. "Much worse for the onlooker," she recalled the tutor saying. It seemed he was right. After a few moments of disorientation, the woman was back spooning porridge in her mouth, albeit a little shakily. It reminded her of her Da trying to eat his Sunday dinner under the flinty eye of her Ma after a skinful in The Harp. It was the only noteworthy incident on the general report submitted to the nursing office at the end of that day. Shelley felt very "nursey" as she recorded the seizure as instructed, the time of the beginning of the seizure, the duration and recovery. No further fits at time of report. Student Nurse Merrigan.

By nine o'clock, all 28 women were up, out of bed, breakfasted and either out of the door to their daily occupation or sitting in the dayroom. The dayroom was a large, airy room with high cathedral ceilings separated from the dining area with teak units and a television bolted onto a high shelf. A radio was now playing *Bye Bye Baby* by the Bay City Rollers. This struck Shelley as so bizarre to hear this song in this alien world that was so far removed from any other place she had ever been. There were high back chairs placed along the walls in rows. They were covered in a plastic green covering suitable for a deft mop up of urine. The women who had no place to go were left behind, all sat alongside each other, all in their own solitary universe. A small woman with Down's syndrome looked intently at her own hand which she flapped in front of her face. Shelley had fed her as she wasn't "self-caring". Henty, a quick moving lady who wore a floral dress and ankle socks was still "playing up" at breakfast, had been given some medication and was now listing in a chair, almost asleep.

"You can make the beds with Nurse Slater and then come to the office," Sister Berry said.

Nurse Slater was an SEN. A State Enrolled Nurse. She had a lazy eye that was magnified behind thick glasses. Shelley wondered how she saw anything at all, her glasses were so filthy. She started to tell Shelley about the patients as they set about making the beds.

"Mary Ryan is a lazy bitch. You have to push her, or she would lay in her stinking bed all day. No doubt she has Irish blood in her," she said, looking at Shelley in a challenging way, as if to provoke a reaction. Shelley was shocked. Having never left home, she had been unprepared for this hostile response to her nationality although her Da had tried to warn her.

"Henty is alright most of the time. You just need to show them who is boss. No spoiling them. You understand? You students coming in with your fancy ideas and all. We know best. Give them an inch and they will soon be out of control. Lunatics running the asylum."

Shelley didn't know what to say. They were the experts, after all. She did not think she had any ideas, fancy or otherwise but she wasn't sure she would ever view the patients in such a disparaging way.

"Oh, don't tell me you are a soft shite. We had another student like that before. Actually kissed that dirty cow Lily on the forehead one night after she had a fit. Does them no good. You are only here three months and then we are stuck with them. Whining and spoilt."

"Oh, I don't think I will be like that," Shelley stammered, and Nurse Slater looked at her. "Hmmm, we'll see. Beds."

Some of the patients had already made their beds, but they had to be made to a certain specification with hospital corners and the openings of the pillows facing away from the dormitory door, so Shelley and Nurse Slater remade them. They placed teddies on each bed as a final touch. "Just in case the nursing officer peers in here when he does his rounds. Stupid if you ask me, but they want a "homely environment", whatever that means. It is a bloody hospital for subnormals."

Already jaded, Shelley stood in front of Sister Berry. She thought she should tell Sister Berry about her disturbing conversation with Nurse Slater. Before she could start, Sister Berry said,

"I want you to shadow Nurse Slater. She is the best worker here and I rely on her completely." Shelley came to learn that Sister Berry was averse to getting her hands dirty and she enjoyed the discipline of the ward when Nurse Slater was on duty. Nurse Slater was unafraid of over medicating the patients for a quiet shift. She disregarded the drug administration sheets and seemed to indiscriminately double up the doses of Largactil at will. The way the patients ducked away from her and got out of slapping distance told Shelley she was also unafraid of hurting the women she was paid to care for. With horror, Shelley understood who was really in charge. Sister Berry would remain complicit as it made her working life much easier. She knew. She bloody well knew. Shelley seethed as she looked at Sister Berry with her neat dark blue Sister's uniform and her clean little white hands. She saw a small smile play around her mouth as Nurse Slater took the slipper Pammy was pleasuring herself with and cracked it around her head. "Dirty bitch," she said, as she whipped herself up into a slapping frenzy. "Dirty, dirty little bitch! Disgusting, filthy little animal!" she shouted. Appearing not to see, Sister Berry walked off towards the office, tucking a little curl that had strayed back under her perfectly styled hair. Shelley felt physically sick. She felt murderous. She had a big family and was used to the odd scuffle. But she was paralysed. Completely immobile. And before she could do anything, everything was as it was before. Nurse Slater was smoothing her dress down and readjusting her hat which had gone askew with her efforts. Pammy was further curled up in her chair. She was silent, not crying, but rocking herself back and forth rhythmically. The radio continued to play. "I'm not in love," 10 cc sang. Shelley was rooted to the spot.

"What's up with you?" Nurse Slater asked, looking at Shelley. "Oh, you going to go crying to your tutor now, are you? Pammy needs to learn she can't do that. Dirty little beast."

Shelley was unable to reply. As if she had imagined it, Nurse Slater said she needed to "do the bundles". This task involved selecting a dress, a cardigan, a vest, and pants, (no bra) for the next morning. She behaved as if she had done nothing untoward and hummed contentedly as she briskly selected the items of clothing for the bundles. At lunchtime, Berry and Slater laughed together at something Shelley did not catch. With an awful clarity, Shelley realised this was how Cypress was run. How could it be? Yet this was lauded as a flagship ward. Clean, homely, with well turned-out and co-operative patients. Civilised mealtimes, in the main. And on a Sunday, when the rare relative made a visit, the patients became "the ladies" sporting a bit of lipstick and blusher and the best the communal clothes stock had to offer. The Nursing Officer was always impressed as he sat down to a bacon sandwich and a cup of tea with Sister and her team and was waited on by Mary Ryan and Henty.

Chapter 9

On her second day, Sister Berry told Shelley that by the end of the placement, she expected Shelley to know the name, age and diagnosis of all 28 patients. Additionally, she needed to do an in-depth study of two of them. The case notes were all in a big metal cabinet in the corner of the office. She fished out the first set of case notes and showed Shelley the general order of the notes. The most contemporaneous notes are at the back, she explained.

Grace Offord.

There was a grainy photo of a woman with dark curls and a round face, smiling at the camera. She was wearing a smart dark dress with a neat white collar. With a jolt of shock, she recognised her as the woman who had the seizure yesterday. Her face was wreathed in little keloid scars - badly sutured - Shelley thought.

Admission 1962. Moderate sub-normality and grand mal epilepsy.

"A relative newcomer!" Sister Berry said.

" The lady who was in the lobby yesterday? Lara?"

"Ah, Lara Demengel. Creeping Jesus, I call her, sneaking around all the time, appearing when you don't expect her. She was on Beech, the locked ward, for years after half killing a nurse during the war.

She was abnormally aggressive back in the day by the sounds of it. Largactil sorted that out! Don't turn your back on her, mind - the Doc thinks she's burnt out, but I still wouldn't trust her by a country mile. I don't hold with her having special treatment and all. A side room, no less, after what she did. Oh no, no dormitory for Miss Demengel. Doctor Winstanley reckons on soft treatment for this lot. She says if we treat them like animals, they will behave like them. Anyway, you can study in the quiet room. Nobody uses it during the day."

Shelley picked up the notes and took them to the quiet room. The quiet room was painted a pale green and was furnished with two chairs that, unlike on the ward, were upholstered in a busy pattern of greens and mauves. A low coffee table covered the expanse between the two chairs. There was a gilt framed picture of a flock of sheep under an avenue of trees in a snowy landscape, which was slightly askew. On the other wall, there was the same scene but with autumn hues. Opening the blue card file on her lap, she noticed the photos clipped to the front leaf. Shelley unclipped them. She gasped as she looked at the same eyes that had stared at her so vacantly yesterday. Long dark hair, unkempt and matted. A sprinkling of freckles. A small, neat mouth. And a small birthmark beneath her right eye. And what looked like a black eye, a real shiner by the look of it. She looked like she had done a few rounds in the ring. None of that could hide that she had been a beauty, albeit untamed.

Admission sheet.

The Mental Deficiency Act 1913

Date: October 30th 1937

Name: Lara Demengel

DOB: November 20th 1921

Age on admission: 16

Status: Formal

Diagnosis:

Moral Defective

Violent (Considered dangerous)

Mute

Feeble minded

Licentious

Ambulant

Continent

Shelley considered the thickness of the notes. There was not much in the way of content considering Lara had been in Wellswood for almost forty years. A lifetime. It was hard to decipher the handwriting in a lot of the entries. There were some typed up pieces of paper pertaining to changes in legislation to the Mental Deficiency Act of 1959, where Lara went from being described as a moral defective to severely subnormal. Shelley rolled the words around in her head. They sounded archaic to her and grated on her new-found sensibilities from her time in introductory block.

The infrequent entries by medics were mostly typewritten, especially the more recent entries by Dr Winstanley who was more diligent than her predecessors. Shelley had heard that Dr Winstanley had brought her progressive ideas from Canada. She was therefore treated with significant suspicion by "the old guard" who were familiar with the regimen of Dr Devonish, who had been the chief medical superintendent since the war. He was known for his casual cruelty to the patients. He performed complete dental clearance for "biters" and stitched head wounds of epileptics without administering local anaesthesia. He said it was akin to veterinary practice. His pernicious attitude permeated through the staff and to attempt to advocate for more humane treatments was to really put your head above the parapet. Any truly altruistic staff left swiftly, rightly judging a systemic change in ethos would be impossible.

Shelley was heartened by Dr Winstanley's gentler approach to practice. The Canadian was taking a keen interest in Lara and was particularly speculative about her apparent mutism. She referenced a nurse's entry from ten years previously. Lara had been noted to sing a few lines from a nursery rhyme. Shelley rifled back to find the entry.

This must have been among the first coach trips from the hospital run by an enthusiastic volunteer, Ken Loftus. Ken had ingratiated himself amongst the patients who were sufficiently able to access his coach and be driven to local beauty spots. The staff welcomed these trips as it meant they could huddle around the tv and watch Crown Court and eat the patients' treats that came up from the stores. The patients weren't allowed off the coach, but Ken's wife Sheila would pack snacks to eat whilst "on board". The radio would blare out tinny renditions of the old hits that the verbal patients would sing along to. Ken would give a running commentary like a bone fide tour guide. A decade later, Ken was a regular fixture of Wellswood and a breath of fresh air to the patients, who would wave and call out to him as he passed like a member of the royal family. It was usually the job of the student and pupil nurses to act as escorts on these outings.

10th June 1965

I was asked to escort the patients on a coach trip to Lusty Glaze beach. I had been told to sit next to Lara as it was her first time on a trip outside of the hospital and on the coach. She appeared to be agitated as she got on the coach but seemed to relax as Ken welcomed everyone on board and handed out cartons of Kia-Ora and Nice biscuits. She sat by the window and pressed her nose up against the pane to look out at the changing countryside. As the coach turned into the track leading to Lusty Glaze, Lara rocked in her chair and sang quietly under her breath, but with clarity.

"Half a pound of tuppenny rice, half a pound of treacle."

Lara didn't say anything else but seemed quite happy and settled.

Student Nurse Theresa Wallis.

So. Not mute as her reports indicated. Absolutely fascinating. She was frustrated by the lack of information in the notes. Shelley leafed through a few more pages of illegible nursing notes, mostly from students flexing their report writing skills. "Report only what you see and hear. No opinions," echoed the voice of her tutor. Then her eyes fixed upon a report from 1972.

August 10th 1972

I was assigned to escort duty during the weekly coach trip with Ken Loftus. We were headed towards a National Trust property to see the gardens. Lara was initially relaxed and co-operative and showed no signs of agitation.

As we drew nearer to our destination, Lara became extremely agitated, she left her seat and refused to sit down. As Ken drove into the gates of Celyn Lodge, Lara became increasingly perturbed. She ran down the aisle of the bus and attempted to prise open the coach doors. Ken stopped the coach. Lara would not return to her seat and was extremely overstimulated. I attempted to prompt her back to her seat. Lara pushed me away and once again tried frantically to open the door. Pupil Nurse Stocker and I had to restrain her on the floor as we urged Ken to return to Wellswood. Upon her return, Nurse Slater administered 50mg Chlorpromazine intramuscular. Lara was more settled at time of report.

Student Nurse Angela Blackledge. (AB)

Shelley wondered what had caused Lara to become so agitated. She was also curious to find any reports on what Sister Berry had said about her previous violence and what lead to such a long spell on the locked ward. Going back in the notes, Shelley found it.

Chapter 10

18th July 1942

Events on the world stage were intensifying as the second world war raged on. Life in Wellswood, however, was much the same, far away from the Blitz. They were insulated from the challenges facing the townsfolk of Mallock and the rest of Cornwall.

There had been an exceptionally hot spell of weather in Cornwall. The large sash windows of Cypress Villa had been opened to let in some air. The chairs had been taken outside on the veranda to allow the patients to sit outside.

Lara was restless. She was hot and longed for respite in the cooling ocean waters. She had not swum for five years. As the midday sun further brightened the day, Lara started to pace up and down along the length of the veranda. Mary Ryan looked flushed in the face as she fussed with her baby doll in its pram. She had also had a baby out of wedlock and had been in Wellswood a few years before Lara. She looked permanently frightened and clung to her doll.

There were two young nurses on duty that morning. They sat on the veranda, stretching their legs out to catch some sunrays.

"This is the life," laughed Nurse Treloar, "Getting paid to sit in the sun!"

"Off duty in an hour too," replied Nurse Fruin as she stretched herself out in the chair, luxuriating in the warmth of the sun. They had been on duty since 7am and were looking forward to a free afternoon, although a nap was on the agenda for Nurse Fruin.

"Sit down Lara, for God's sake. You are blocking the sun."

Lara did not desist and carried on her pacing, like a caged animal. Her agitation was palpable.

Mary Ryan had just placed her baby doll in its pram. Tenderly, she covered her over with a woolen blanket, making soothing sounds and pulling up the hood of the pram to protect the doll from the sun.

"Oh, is baby going to sleep now," mocked Nurse Treloar. Nurse Fruin snorted a laugh.

Mary dropped her gaze.

"Aw, baby girl needs a sleep after her milk," echoed Nurse Fruin, picking up on the theme.

Mary's lip began to tremble, and she looked around anxiously, at a loss as to what to do. She stood stock-still. Without getting up, Nurse Treloar hooked her foot under the handle of the pram and tipped it up. The doll fell onto the ground.

"Oh, poor baby is dead," they said together, as Mary looked forlornly at the scrubby patch of grass where her doll lay, looking unblinkingly at the sky. The laughter stopped abruptly as Lara picked up the doll and brushed the grass off before handing it back to Mary, who clutched it tightly to her chest. With lightning speed, Lara launched herself at Nurse Treloar, circled her neck with her hands and began to violently choke her. Mirth over, Nurse Fruin tried to extricate Lara's grip from around her neck. Lara pushed her off with ease and tightened her grip. Nurse Treloar struggled to no avail. She was no match for Lara's kinetic energy, fuelled by blind rage. By the time help arrived in the form of six attendants from various wards, Nurse Treloar was slumped in the chair she had been enjoying so much just brief moments before, as if dead.

Lara was taken to Beech ward. The heavy doors of the strong room were slammed shut behind her. There was an ultrathin bare mattress on the floor. She lowered herself gingerly onto it, trying to find the least painful position to avoid pressure on the extensive bruising sustained during her "restraint". As the barbiturates started to take effect, Lara replayed the scene in her mind. She remembered the feel of Nurse Treloar's neck as she squeezed relentlessly, her veins throbbing against the tightening vice grip around her throat. She recalled Mary Ryan's look of bewilderment and then gratitude, as she handed the doll to her. As the last vestiges of consciousness left her, she smiled.

Chapter 11

Shelley put down the notes. No wonder Doctor Winstanley was showing such an interest in Lara. Seeing Lara drift around the ward, almost ethereally, it seemed hard to reconcile the girl who was capable of such a frenzied attack with the strange, vacant figure of today. What was behind the attack? Why would she spontaneously assault a nurse without any apparent reason? The reports said Lara had been agitated and uncooperative all day and had attacked Nurse Treloar impulsively. Shelley also reflected on the penalty Lara had paid; twenty years on Beech. Shelley had visited Beech on her orientation morning to the hospital. She had been wearing her nurse's hat. The ward sister had asked if she would like to take it off herself or have it torn off in three seconds flat by the patients.

Shelley had been terrified as she walked through the locked doors and made her way through a maze of twisted humanity. Some of the women were naked. "Strippers," explained the Staff Nurse, meaning they tore off their clothes. One woman was wearing what looked like a nylon smock with her arms pinned to her sides. Ties were fastened around the back. "A strong suit," the Staff Nurse said by way of explanation.

The ward had a large table and chairs which were fastened to the floor to prevent them being used as missiles. Shelley looked for some semblance of humanity. One of the women walked on all fours and another seemed entranced by twirling what looked like a dishcloth before her eyes. They all seemed to be rocking rhythmically, either backwards and forwards or from side to side. The atmosphere was tense; it was like waiting for a dormant volcano to erupt at any time. Despite Shelley's best efforts, she could not get rid of the stench from her nostrils for days. And once again, those inhuman sounds. She was sure only someone who had ever been to Beech would ever be able to know what she meant. Her best description was to compare it to the sound of lowing cattle combined with the screams of a maternity ward. Shelley likened the scene to a depiction of hell she had seen once in the library in an art history book by Hieronymus Bosch. Beech was not a teaching ward so Shelley would not have to do a placement there which was a huge relief to her.

Returning the notes to the filing cabinet, Shelley resolved to attempt a further interaction with Lara. On her way to the office, she saw Nurse Slater dragging a screeching Eva Shaberman by the wrist towards the washrooms. Eva was naked from the waist down and covered in excrement. Shelley retched with the smell.

"Oh, look at Student Nurse la di da, all nice and prissy in the quiet room whilst the rest of us have to work. Bone idle students. You are all the same. Noses deep in case notes at the first sign of a shitty arse."

Reddening, Shelley told Nurse Slater's retreating rigid back that she had been told to read case notes. She could hear Eva's shrieks as they echoed down the cavernous corridor, incited to go faster by Nurse Slater slapping the back of her head. As she turned to open the office door, there was Lara, standing behind her. Still, soundless. Shelley remembered Sister Berry calling her creeping Jesus and realised she did indeed seem to materialise out of thin air. Lara looked at Shelley intently. Again, she couldn't tell whether Lara was completely vacant or fully sentient. She held Shelley's gaze momentarily before looking back towards where Eva and Nurse Slater had disappeared.

"Lara?" Shelley ventured, but Lara turned away without acknowledgement and evaporated down the dormitory towards her single side room, the one Sister Berry had spoken of as if it were the honeymoon suite at the Ritz.

Chapter 12

Once again, Shelley was in the quiet room with Lara's case notes open. She wanted to know what had happened to Lara's baby. Shelley went back to the time of admission to see what she could discover about the circumstances of the birth.

In the photo on the fly of her case notes, Lara had a black eye and looked unkempt. There was no date of birth for the child, so Shelley had no way of knowing Lara had been admitted so soon after giving birth. Or that she had fought the men who had brought her in to Wellswood under heavy guard like a wild cat. She got the black eye from one of the men who had punched her roundly after Lara had caught him with a painful scratch to his neck. He was not a man who had any sensibilities towards the fairer sex, as his wife, Ruthie Bell, would have been able to attest every Saturday morning after he had a heavy night at "The Rose". Shelley wondered at the family who had apparently abdicated all responsibility for Lara. She thought how lucky she had been not to have been similarly caught out herself in that way. She remembered her friend Niamh who had found herself pregnant at fifteen and had become something of a pariah back home. The Shaughnessy's had moved to get away from the stares and the hushed whispers of judgement. But her family had stuck by her, resisting the pressures to send her away to the Sisters of Mercy and they raised the child together. Niamh had written to Shelley and enclosed a polaroid of a sweet looking little girl in a wheelbarrow being pushed by a doting grandfather.

So, who were the Demengels? Why had none of them visited Lara in almost forty years? What had happened to the baby? When did Lara stop talking? Frustrated by the lack of information in the notes, she resolved to speak to Dr Winstanley to try and uncover some more history. Did she know more? Could Lara herself provide any clues to her past? Shelley was not optimistic; Lara did not seem to see Shelley at all.

Lara did see her. She saw everything and everyone. She saw Nurse Slater as a black cloud, a dark presence, as she performed all her duties with a malevolent precision. She saw every little slap, every push, every sharp pinch. She heard all her mocking of the patients, the teasing and the winding up. Nurse Slater knew all their vulnerabilities and what would send them "up the pole" with a quiet whisper in their ears. She saw the cloud infect every corner of the ward; there was no escape. Some of the ladies tried to be invisible, curled up extra tightly to keep out of her way. They automatically cowered as the cloud approached, hoping she had expended her passion for cruelty on someone else and her energy was depleted. She saw her whispering in Henty's ear which would lead her to go and pull Pammy's hair, making Pammy look around in confusion and cry out. This amused the black cloud, and she would reward Henty with some chocolate and some respite of her own for a few hours. Lara saw her striding across the lawn purposefully towards Cypress before a shift, ready for another day of sport. She saw her at the medication trolley liberally pouring out sedatives without measure, to give herself a quiet shift in the mornings. She would see her wrap her coat around her as she left, satiated for the day. She heard the palpable, collective sigh of relief as the cloud entered the night.

Lara had seen Sister Berry on her first day as ward sister five years before. She saw how neat and careful she was. Everything about her was meticulous. Even her regulation navy blue sisters' uniform was embellished with non-regulation touches. A starched white collar and frothy puffed sleeves, the type worn by prestigious paediatric nurses in the London hospitals. Her dark hair was coiled tidily under her cap and held in place by multiple kirby grips. It was Sister Berry who introduced the whole tablecloths and teapots ideas to Cypress, as if she were presiding over a Lyons teashop. But she was weak. Lara saw that. Nurse Slater quickly went to work eroding any semblance of the good intentions she had started off with. She failed to act when she saw Nurse Slater pull Eva's head back by her hair to brush her teeth. Incrementally, Nurse Slater demonstrated how sadistic she could be, and Sister did nothing. Not only did she not stop her, but Lara had also seen her try and conceal a smirk or stifle a laugh at some of the teasing. She saw Nurse Slater recounting some story or other to her in the office and their shared delight in some act of cruelty or degradation. They would encourage slavish devotion from some of the ladies by making them "pet for the day". They would bestow some kindnesses, usually in the form of sweets and allowing them to help give out medications or serve at table to the visiting nursing officers. Sister Berry would take a back seat and enjoy some proxy physical punishments meted out by the day's "chosen one" to the more defenseless patients. The patients did this with no small relief knowing that tomorrow, in all probability, they would likely be the target of this twisted game.

She saw them both scurrying to present a calm and clean villa before the morning round by the nursing officer. Lara saw Mr. Scott as he trundled towards Cypress. He came every morning on the pretense of an inspection. Lara saw this was always the last villa on his rounds where he would be fortified with tea and a sandwich with a few choice pieces of bacon held back from the patients' breakfast. He would be waited on, usually by Henty and Mary Ryan and he would compliment the staff on the "normalisation of the environment" and the placidity of the patients. Lara saw the bacon fat run down his chin and drop onto the knot of his tie. Sister Berry would beam with pride and heap praise on Nurse Slater and whichever nursing assistant was on duty. Lara saw he was blind and deaf and would not be their rescuer.

Lara was weighing Shelley up. Her hopes had faded at the sight of Eva disappearing into the bathrooms, her screams ignored. Lara had a glimmer of hope some years back that had been quickly extinguished. There had been a young student nurse who had tenderly kissed Lily on the forehead after she had a fit. They had drummed her out. When she left, Lara's hopes had gone with her.

However, Lara was omitted from Nurse Slater's little diversions. She was neither selected as pet nor target. The staff were wary of her. She had almost killed a nurse and had ended her career. Despite her advancing years, she remained strong in body and there was an element of uncertainty about her. Besides, there were plenty of easy targets to amuse the staff. Why take any unnecessary risks of retaliation? Consequently, Lara was largely ignored and left to her own devices. Unlike many on the ward, she was able to attend to her own personal care needs. She did not join the morning queue of naked bodies waiting for the same bath.

The morning ritual reminded Shelley of the sheep dips she had seen at home. What shocked her most was how quickly she became accustomed to it and could see how effective the method was for speed and ease. She recalled her horror at seeing so much nakedness at the same time. Despite coming from a big family, they were modest about exposing their nudity and Shelley realised with some surprise that the only pubic hair she had seen was her own, including Callum, as all their fumblings had been committed in the dark. "Dehumanisation" was how her textbook described it. One nurse would preside over the bath and another was tasked with drying the patients with threadbare, damp towels with no attention to details such as in between toes or behind ears. It was all perfunctory, performed with an absence of any sense of dignity or privacy. This focus on task was how so much was accomplished by 9 am and facilitated a leisurely staff breakfast soon after.

Lara took her time in the bathroom. She bathed alone. The water temperature was regulated to prevent scalding so there was no opportunity for a hot bath. The bath was filled for her with a meagre few inches of tepid water and the procedure was overseen, usually by a nursing assistant. She missed the melee of the pre-breakfast rush hour and to the irritation of her attendant, she would linger in her ablutions. The other daily ritual Lara managed to evade was the daily B.O. book, staring blankly if the uninitiated deigned to ask her whether she had opened her bowels. One of the student's tasks was to ask the patients daily if their bowels had opened. Shelley had only encountered the B.O. acronym in relation to soap adverts and was a mite surprised that the patients were not only familiar with the term but also able to report if they had "been" with no sense of embarrassment. Some patients were able to elaborate and provide some additional embellishments from a simple yes or no. "A good turnout" seemed to be the most common bolt on information that Shelley would dutifully write in the notebook. Shelley wrote in her first letter home "Ma, every shit is written in a book," but it had now become so embedded in her daily duties, she no longer gave it any thought whilst dutifully collating this daily record.

Similarly, the "Menses" book needed to be filled in every time someone started to menstruate. There was little else to write about, Shelley supposed. Although Sister Berry said it was of clinical import, particularly in relation to constipation and epilepsy. It also informed who would need to undertake some mechanical assistance on "enema day". On Cypress this took place on a Thursday, with everyone unable to report a motion being subjected to either an enema or suppositories, usually immediately after the staff breakfast in the morning.

Shelley had been on Cypress for a month. She was starting to formulate her case study on Lara and Sister Berry had given her permission to spend more time with her. So, it was on this morning that Shelley drew her bath and went to her little side room to say her bath was ready. She had popped in some Radox bubble bath from the stores and run a much deeper than regulation bath for her. Lara was rummaging in her bedside cabinet drawer when she was startled by a sound, one she hadn't heard for years. A gentle knock on her bedroom door. Nobody had knocked on her door for years: staff barged in whenever they chose.

"Lara, I have run you a bath." Lara looked at her quizzically. She was Irish, she knew that much, as she had heard Berry and Slater calling her the lumpen Irish one. She hadn't seen much of her as she had spent more time than most in the quiet room. She hadn't yet partaken in any cruelties herself, but she hadn't opposed them either. To Lara, she was unchartered waters. Large but ineffective, struck dumb by the horrors and immobilised by fear.

Lara padded behind Shelley to the bathroom. She was surprised to see a deep bath but not surprised to find, beneath the blanket of bubbles, the water was tepid. Not without envy, Shelley noticed that Lara's physique was of a young girl still, despite being in her early 50's. The only telltale sign that she was a mother, was an intricate network of lines across her abdomen, like those left on ice after being skated upon.

The silence in the cavernous bathroom was unbearable. Shelley was desperate to feign an ease she did not feel. She knew asking Lara questions was fruitless, but she was desperate to try and make a connection. To build a "rapport", as she had been taught in block. She wanted to distance herself from the other staff, to somehow transmit good person vibes to Lara. She recalled the astounding entry in Lara's notes that she had sung "half a pound of tuppeny rice" on that first coach trip. Hesitantly, she started to hum the tune, quietly, in case other staff heard, and she became the butt of their scorn. It sounded tinny and alien to her own ears, but she persisted, as it felt more comfortable than the silence. Having penetrated the stifling quiet, Shelley decided she would just talk. She started talking about home, her family and the beauty of Wicklow. It felt good, and she realised with a jolt how lonely she had been since arriving at Wellswood and how foreign she felt in this peculiar place. It was if the brakes were off and Shelley garbled on, so much so that she failed to notice Lara was loosely paying attention, transported back to a warm kitchen next to Nancy, chuntering on about nothing of any importance but liking the sound and the feeling of safety it gave her. Shelley broke off her story about coming to Cornwall to get away from a broken heart. She didn't think Lara needed to hear about Mr. O'Hare.

"Do you want your back doing Lara?" She had no way of knowing that nobody had touched her with any tenderness since Nancy in 1937. After some moments Lara leant forward and allowed Shelley to wash her back as she went back to chatting about whatever; Lara had ceased to listen to the words but was only focused on the tune; the lilt of her voice and the warmth of her tone. She passed Lara the towel and said "Sure, you will want to be doing this by yourself" and left her to finish off in privacy.

Later, she passed the quiet room and saw Shelley looking intently at a file, a frown making an intersection between her eyes. Lara decided to wait watchfully before writing this one off.

Shelley decided she would try and catch Dr Winstanley to beef up her case study. There was so little to go on because of the scarcity of information in the notes and Lara was clearly unable to offer anything in the way of history. She had pondered about changing her subject to Olivia, who had Down syndrome and had a family who visited monthly. It would be an easy win to expound the physical characteristics of those with Down syndrome and speak to Olivia's family about her delayed milestones and early childhood. But Lara piqued her interest. Her notes raised more questions than they answered. She was intrigued by her quietude and the seeming trepidation she elicited from even Nurse Slater. There was the obvious incarceration on Beech for her attack on Nurse Treloar. The anecdotal tale passed down through the annals of Wellswood history was that Nurse Treloar never returned to work. Her voice was permanently altered by the attack and she had become nervy and reclusive. She was cared for by her elderly parents in Mallock until they died. After some months, a relative raised concern about her ability to be independent and she was moved into a long stay ward herself in the main hospital in Bodmin, or so the story went. Nobody seemed to know if she were dead or alive. Nurse Fruin strenuously denied ever having been a close friend or ally, with a convenient amnesia about all the intimacies they had shared and their mutual predilection for hectoring and harassing those they should have been caring for. Nurse Fruin continued to work at Wellswood until 1962. She had learned a valuable lesson that fateful day and tried to exercise more moral treatment of the patients. She felt guilty that Lara was languishing on Beech but not enough to exonerate her by admitting the provocation by herself and Nurse Treloar. Six years later in 1968 as she lay on her deathbed riddled with cancer, she prayed for God to forgive her for her sins against Mary Ryan, Lara Demengel and the countless other faceless and nameless patients she had maltreated over the years.

Chapter 13

Shelley flushed red as she remembered Dr Winstanley telling her to lose weight at her pre-nursing medical as she walked up the concrete ramp to Cherry. She had managed to lose a few pounds, but this had been regained quickly, plus a few extra for good measure. She had not seen a fresh vegetable since leaving Wicklow. She had made a special friend of Maisie who served up the daily stodge in the hospital canteen. Maisie seemed determined not to allow Shelley to dip beneath 13 stone and winked as she gave her double portions. Something and chips every day. She supplemented this with snacks bought at the hospital shop. She loathed herself for her appetite and cursed herself for not being more disciplined as she knocked on the door to the doctor's office.

"Oh shit," Dr Winstanley exclaimed as she waved cigarette smoke away through the small sliver of open window. She had clearly not been expecting anyone. She was disappointed that smoking in the office was no longer deemed acceptable. She still did it but not with the freedom she had enjoyed previously. Not all changes are good she mused.

"Ah, Shelley, isn't it? From Wicklow. I always remember us outsiders! Come in. Sit down. Don't stand on ceremony. You're making me nervous."

Shelley noticed a photograph of a laughing child, maybe four years old, propped up in front of a stack of books. A boy in a red and white striped t-shirt and blue shorts.

"Is that your son?" Shelley asked.

"Oh yes. When he was still a human! He's a teenager now. We don't even speak the same language. He talks in grunts," she laughed. "Now what can I do for you?"

"I am on my first placement on Cypress. I expect you know I must do a case study on one of the patients. I want to do it on Lara Demengel."

Dr Winstanley sat back in her seat and whistled through the pen she was holding. Sizing Shelley up, she asked how things were on Cypress ward? How was she getting on with the staff? Was she fitting in? Shelley's lips tightened and she felt herself feel suddenly hot and uncomfortable. Studiously avoiding her gaze, she looked down and examined the chair leg. After a brief interlude, Dr Winstanley let out a breath.

"Oh sod it," the older woman said, and opened her carton of cigarettes. She pulled one out between her teeth. She lit it and fanned the smoke away ineffectively. Shelley gave a little cough.

"Shelley, can I make this easier for you sweetie?" She said this so unexpectedly gently that Shelley felt the unwelcome prick of tears in her eyes and the familiar constriction of her throat consistent with fruitless efforts to stem sobs.

She went on. "I have had my concerns about Cypress for some time. All that bullshit about a homely environment and a harmonious little outfit. That noxious witch Berry does not fool me for a second, in her pristine uniform and the rehearsed phrases she trots out to that imbecile, Scott." Taking a deep inhalation of her cigarette, she got into her stride. "Lazy bastard is counting down the days to his retirement, plus he is simply enthralled by the sight of her wiggling and fawning in front of him in her pimped-up uniform. He has sold his soul for a piece of skirt and a pig sandwich. Useless, pathetic man. As for that psychopath, Slater..."

Dr Winstanley stopped as Shelley had begun to cry as if she would never stop. It was a mixture of relief that there was some humanity to be found in this place and guilt that she had seen it and failed to do anything. She waited patiently for the sobs to subside.

"Shelley," she continued, "I have my suspicions, but absolutely no evidence of what goes on within those walls. I have examined the breaks and bruises. I see the women cower as I go to tend to them. I have seen the accident book. The injuries and the purported incidents do not add up. Why do you think I am so hated? I ask questions. I turn up unannounced at odd times. I make myself visible. But nobody is prepared to stand up to this regime. The women that could tell me, don't. Or won't. Or can't. And any staff member with a shred of decency does not last. There is a conspiracy of silence that has lasted for years. I want to stop it. But I cannot without proof. I need help, Shelley."

Shelley looked dumbly at the floor.

"Have you seen anything untoward, Shelley?"

She let out another loud sob which she tried to smother with her trembling hand.

Dr Winstanley handed her a tissue and extinguished her cigarette in the lid of a coffee jar. She sat back and waited. Shelley recovered herself and muttered a quiet "Yes."

"Good girl, good girl," she said, and squeezed Shelley's hand. "Can you help me?"

Shelley lifted her eyes and met the earnestly searching eyes of Dr Winstanley. She nodded her agreement.

"And Lara? My case study?"

"That gives me a perfect excuse to come to Cypress. We can do a little detective work together. I will meet you at Cypress tomorrow."

Chapter 14

With breakfast over, Shelley was in the dormitory making the beds with Nurse Slater when Dr Winstanley breezed into the villa.

Under her breath, Nurse Slater bemoaned her arrival. "Oh, what does that do-gooding bitch want now? Doesn't do any good. She has got no idea what it's like to be here on the ward, day in day out. She doesn't have to deal with them all going up the pole. Bet she has never wiped a shitty arse in her life! Flounces in and thinks she knows what's best for everyone. I wish she would bugger off back to her own country."

Snapping a bedsheet into submission, she ran off to warn Sister Berry that Dr Winstanley was nosing around.

Dr Winstanley said good morning to Shelley who gave a cautious smile in return.

"Ah, Dr Winstanley. A very good morning to you. Can I get you a coffee? Black, no sugar?" asked Sister Berry, her saccharine smile lacking any depth or warmth.

Seeing Shelley, she ordered her to get the doctor a coffee. All that was missing was a click of the fingers.

"Shall we?" Sister Berry said, gesturing towards the office.

"Actually, it's Shelley I've come to see. Perhaps we could use the quiet room? A coffee would be great, thank you, and would you bring me Lara Demengel's case notes?"

Sister Berry rapidly concealed her outrage as she went into the nurse's office to fetch the notes and to rustle up some coffee from the kitchen. She was livid that she was making Student Nurse Merrigan a beverage. The great lumbering Irish girl. Who on earth did she think she was? She would find a way of making her pay later. But she smiled sweetly as Henty brought them coffee and biscuits on a tray while she opened the door.

"Here you are ladies. I will need Shelley at 12.15 to serve lunch, Dr Winstanley. If you can spare her of course!"

Dr Winstanley rolled her eyes as she closed the door on them.

"Phoney bitch," she said, and Shelley allowed herself a smile, now getting used to her un-Doctoresque language.

The agreement was uncomplicated. Shelley would keep a log of every incident that occurred on the ward. She was instructed to write down everything she saw with as much accuracy as possible. She should record the who, what, when and how situations on the ward as soon as possible after they had unfolded and pass this on to the doctor. Shelley was to tell nobody else at this juncture. Not her tutor, not her fellow students. She was not to write home about it. She had two months left on Cypress before her next block. Unless there was an imminent risk to one of the patients, Shelley must not show her hand. She was neither to condone nor condemn any teasing, or mocking, or assaultive behaviour. Only to closely observe, and record. All this in addition to formulating her first placement case study.

"Shall we call Lara in," she said. It was not a question. Shelley had no idea that the doctor intended to speak to Lara, but she went and got her from her side room without any query. She knocked on Lara's door. The door was opened abruptly by Sister Berry. Lara was sitting on her bed looking blankly at an array of sweets, packets of tights and toiletries fresh from the stores that were fanned across her bedspread. She had a half-eaten Caramac in her hand, the golden wrapper catching the sunlight pouring in through the sash window.

"Dr Winstanley wants to speak to Lara," stammered Shelley, unsure what to make of the scene before her.

"Of course she does. Perhaps she would like me to bring her in on a silver platter? Off you go Lara. Don't dawdle dear."

Glaring at Shelley, she brushed past and bristled as she stomped through the dormitory back to her office, almost combusting with hostility. Lara followed Shelley to the quiet room.

"Well, hello, Lara. Come in, come in. Sit down."

Lara didn't sit. She stood, and glowered at Shelley.

"Lara, Shelley is going to sit in with us today if that's okay. She wants to get to know you a little better. And she is going to help me."

Still looking at Shelley with some suspicion, she sat down. Shelley was struck by the ease with which Dr Winstanley spoke to Lara who visibly relaxed as she carried on talking. After a few moments, Lara looked almost comfortable. This, she thought, was finally the therapeutic alliance she had heard of. Dr Winstanley had managed to gain some semblance of trust from

Lara. She thought of her brother Tommy who had liberated a feral cat from the Doherty farm. That cat eventually followed Tommy around like a docile kitty but would hiss and scratch at anyone else who tried to approach her. She spoke to Lara as if she expected her to understand. She did not speak to her as if she had any cognitive difficulties at all, with an assumption she had the capacity to comprehend. Shelley noticed she didn't ask Lara any direct questions that required an answer.

"Well Lara. I expect you are curious as to why myself and Shelley here have asked to talk to you this morning?"

Shelley noted Dr Winstanley dropped her student Nurse title. Irrationally she worried over this momentarily, thinking about what Sister Berry and Nurse Slater would say at this over familiarity. She relaxed as she reminded herself that Lara was mute so she wouldn't be exposed in this way. Dr Winstanley believed in a flat hierarchy. "Unless I am dealing with complete idiots," she later revealed.

"Help yourself to a biscuit, Lara," she continued.

Lara quickly glanced at the biscuits. Good ones. The ones the staff ate when they gathered around the tv in the evening on Wednesdays, to watch that programme they all loved. The one with the cat in a back alley. The tune was a cue for Lara to go to Mary Ryan's bed and pick up the little doll that had lain there for years and take it to her room. She knew she had a little time whilst everyone was glued to the tv. She cradled the doll tightly and gently kissed her head with the tufts of brown nylon hair, now sparse after years of fussing, exposing her plastic scalp. She would fashion a little nest for the doll with her top blanket, shielding her from the elements and keeping her cocooned from harm. And oh, so quietly, she would whisper into her tiny little shell of an ear. "Half a pound of tuppeny rice, half a pound of treacle."

Shelley noted Lara did not take a biscuit and presumed she did not understand the offer.

"Today, Lara, I am going to show you some pictures of all kinds of different objects. I would like to understand you better so I can help you. I hope that makes some sense. Could you point or look at the right picture when I give the word. I will give you a little example to help you," the doctor said. She had placed twelve picture cards on the table and pointed to an apple.

"So, Lara, I am pointing to the apple. So that is how it works. Can you show me the bed?"

Nothing. Lara sat rigid with her unfathomable face giving nothing away. After what felt like an eternity to Shelley, Lara reached out and picked up one of the cards. Without looking at either of the women and clutching the card tightly, Lara slipped out of the quiet room.

"She took the baby! She did it! I was looking for any kind of response to that. That's amazing Shelley; did you see that?"

Shelley was not convinced it was anything significant. She thought it might just as easily have been the picture of the train or the cat she picked up. But not wanting to dampen the older woman's enthusiasm, she agreed there might be something in it.

"I will be back on Friday. Be sure and let Lara know. Keep talking to her, Shelley. Assume she understands.

She does not trust you. Remember she has been treated really, really badly in this shit hole. She is waiting for you to screw up. Tell her what you're doing, like a running commentary. It will help that you came into the session this morning, that I have given you my endorsement. I haven't asked anyone else into my sessions with her so she will know you have my seal of approval. She is weighing me up too, but the fact she hasn't twatted me yet, I am taking as a positive! And Shelley, do try and not look so sketchy around her! Don't be fearful. What's the worst that can happen?"

"She nearly killed a nurse?"

"That was years ago. She was young and strong. Lara is burnt out by now; the institution will have knocked anything out that age left behind. Relax. Bet your bottom dollar that nurse did something to provoke her too. Be kind. She will pick up on your energy."

"But the others? Nurse Slater and the rest?"

"Shelley, I'm assuming you are a Catholic, right?"

Unsure where this was headed, she confirmed she was.

"Well believe it or not, so was I. Once. Bottom line, you know the difference between right and wrong. And one day, you will have to give an account of all you did whilst here. And what you did not do. Standing by and doing nothing makes you as guilty as them. Think carefully about your choices, Shelley".

Pulling a cigarette out with her teeth, she lit it in the foyer before opening the large double doors and making her way back to Cherry.

Chapter 15

The patients who worked were streaming towards the ward for lunch. There was always a hot meal at lunchtime followed by sandwiches and cake at teatime.

"Hello Nurse" a few of them said as they passed Shelley. It was a bright day, but cold. Shelley thought that her Ma would be insisting on a hat, gloves and a scarf for everyone. But the patients didn't have such accessories to keep them warm. They did not complain. They came in with purple hands fumbling with their buttons, eager for food. It was a long time between breakfast and lunch with nothing to snack on, even if they were hungry.

"Don't stand there gormless," Nurse Slater shouted to Shelley, "Feed the babies!"

Shelley picked up two bowls of "soft". The "babies" were on a soft diet. This was a liquidised mass of green, brown and white which Shelley understood to be mash, peas and some kind of meat. Nothing would induce her to try it. For the first time in her life Shelley identified a food that even she would not eat. It looked the same every day. For tea, they had cake softened with milk from the large milk dispenser in the kitchen.

She started to feed Pammy, who opened her mouth up like a little bird Shelley thought. She poured some tea into her mouth from the white plastic beaker with a little spout. She looked dehydrated and her breath smelled sour. Shelley wondered about the quality of her life. Pammy could not talk. She was practically blind although she had enough sense to cower when Nurse Slater came close. She spent all day, every day, in her molded plastic chair. She had an enema once a week. And she was fed slop. She wondered whether she liked music, as the radio was on all day until 6pm when the telly went on. She rocked in her chair forwards and backwards all day. Self-stimulation according to her Tutor. Shelley thought about the masturbation, how primal an activity that must be. Pammy was not the only one who was given to this carnal activity when Nurse Slater wasn't around to police this particular act. Shelley fleetingly thought of what her Ma and Father Quinn would say and laughed to herself. Perhaps she wouldn't write home about that.

Lara was sat on the "spoon's table". This was the table where they could eat with a spoon but could not manage a knife and fork. The patients ate quickly and furtively. Coming from a big family, Shelley recognised this trait; if you weren't careful, Tommy or Ed would nick the chips off your plate and would still be hovering about in the vain hope of leftovers.

"You'd think you were half starved," her Ma would complain.

Grace had almost eaten her lunch and then pinched a piece of gammon from Lily's plate.

"Pincher, pincher!" Henty shouted from the next table. Louder now. "Pincher, Nurse Slater."

Nurse Slater quickly weaved her way through the tables to the serving hatch where there was a big ladle ready for custard. She slapped the ladle in her hand as if assessing its suitability for the job.

Grace did not have time to flinch as Nurse Slater rained blows down on her head with the ladle.

"Greedy little bitch," she said, as Grace slid to the floor, pulling her plate and the remains of her meal on top of her. The ladle caught her on the side of the temple which bled profusely. The sight of the blood streaming from her head created a brief hiatus. The rest of the patients put their heads down and finished their meals, fearing she was now fired up and not yet spent. They knew Nurse Slater fair exhausted herself on occasion and often did not stop until she was breathless with exertion.

"Go and get a towel Merrigan," she ordered. As Shelley rushed to the bathroom, she missed Nurse Slater draw her foot back and land a swift donkey kick to Grace's ribs. She was about to kick her again when Sister Berry called out with some urgency.

"Jean, stop!"

She stopped in surprise and disappointment; she was not yet finished. Sister Berry had never intervened before. Nurse Slater followed Sister's gaze. Dr Winstanley was making her way back across the grass to the Villa. She had only just left and was not due back until Friday.

"Get this mess sorted," she hissed to Nurse Slater. "I will tell her she has had a bad fit and hit her head on the table on the way down. And her side."

Sister Berry intercepted the Doctor in the foyer.

"Back so soon Doctor?" she asked.

"I forgot my scarf. I think I must have left it in the quiet room."

"Well, it just so happens we need you. What fortuitous timing. Poor Grace has just had a nasty seizure and has sustained some injuries in the fall. Nurse Slater and the student nurse are seeing to her now. I can bring her to the clinic room for you once they have cleaned her up. She might need a few sutures. Poor old girl. Her fits seem to be becoming more frequent. Perhaps she needs an increase in her Epilim? Anyway, I will leave that with you. As the doctor of course. Let me go and see where they are."

Sister Berry went back to the chaos of the dining room. She felt an unaccustomed flash of irritation for Nurse Slater's bad timing. What if the Doctor had seen her delivering that kick in the ribs? What if she had caught the flush of illicit delight in her own face as her foot slammed into her side. She needed to be much more careful. She would need to speak to her later. The doctor only worked office hours. Plenty of time to enjoy themselves when she was safely off site.

"Henty, Mary, help Nurse with all this lot. Clear the tables and get the babies back to their seats. Good girl, Henty," she said, fishing a Quality Street out of her pocket and giving it to Henty. Mary looked on enviously.

To Shelley, she raised her finger to her mouth in the universal symbol for silence.

Sister Berry and Nurse Slater flanked Grace as they lead her to the clinic room, bleeding, and clutching her side.

Later, Shelley read the daily Nurses report.

12.30

Grace suffered a grand mal seizure. Sustained a wound to her right temple and bruising to her right ribs as she fell. Seen by Dr Winstanley. Three sutures inserted into head wound and prescribed paracetamol PRN (whenever necessary) re: pain from injury to chest area. Sodium Valproate increased to 200mg tds (Three times daily) with immediate effect. No further seizures at time of report.

Signed. Sister Berry

"Shall I give Grace some paracetamol Nurse Berry? She is holding her side and grimacing." Shelley asked later.

"I am not sure who you think you are, Merrigan. I am in charge of medication, and I decide who gets what, and when. And while we are at it, I don't know what you think you saw at lunchtime. We can't have that kind of disorder at table. Grace should know better. It will go very badly for you if you were to talk about anything about Cypress to anyone. We enjoy a reputation as the best of Wellswood and I intend it to stay that way. Mr. Scott and Mr. Devonish are old friends. You have seen how satisfied Mr. Scott is with our good work every day. You simply would not be believed. I can be the making or the breaking of you here, Merrigan. One word from me and you will be hightailing it back to the bogs of Ireland and you will never nurse again. Do you understand?"

Shelley had never felt so intimidated. She had brawled in the lounge with Tommy once when he had teased her about having a crush on Brendan Kelly when she was twelve. Tommy had been amused and secretly proud of how she had been able to give him a bit of a hiding. She could slug it out with the best of them. A Merrigan for sure.

So why did she feel so frightened of this petite, neat and smooth-talking ward Sister. She could flatten her for sure, no problem. Why did she find her so menacing, maybe even more so than Slater?

"I understand," she replied dully.

Exhausted, Shelley returned to her room that evening. She lay on the bed and looked at the ceiling. She was too tired to move so she ignored the knock on the door.

"Shelley, answer the door, would you? It's Julie. I just saw you go in, so I know you are there."

Julie came from Mallock and could have lived out but said it was the best chance of leaving her strict family and to have a bit of a laugh.

"Come on, we're going to the social club. I am on a late tomorrow, so I'm going to get pissed. And try and get off with Gerry," she laughed.

"Thanks Julie but I am banjaxed. Maybe Friday. Payday disco?"

After a few more attempts, Julie gave up. "Friday for definite then," and she heard the sounds of voices and laughter retreating down the corridor. They seemed so carefree and untainted by the horrors of Wellswood. She wondered if Julie had seen anything like the horrors she had witnessed on Cypress and whether she would idly watch or whether she had a backbone. Miserably, Shelley took her notebook from under her mattress and began to write everything that happened that day. She felt wretched and ashamed as again she had not intervened. She had avoided seeing the doctor after she had finished stitching Grace up. She had busied herself doing the bundles, until she heard her leave the villa.

She remembered the doctor's words to her as she tried to recall every detail.

"You need to document the tail end of a fart," she had said. Shelley wondered what good it all would do. She felt so torn. She could just pretend it hadn't happened and move on to her next placement with a good report. Cypress had, after all, been run like that for years. Was it really so awful? The patients were fed and watered, had shelter and were clean. They must be used to it by now. It was one of the wards on the approved visiting list whenever any local dignitaries were being shown around. Crucially, it was a teaching ward and had been since Sister Berry started five years before. That meant several students had completed their placements without any concerns being raised. Why should she risk it all? To go back to Ireland in disgrace with a bad reference? Maybe to have to get a job in Kelly's garage and sell Mars bars all day. And to have to see Connor O'Hare again, with her nursing dreams in tatters.

She thought of Grace lying on the cold dining room floor with blood streaming from the livid cut on her temple. She had looked pale and dazed, with the stolen bit of gammon beside her and mashed potato and gravy spilled down the front of her dress. Sighing, she picked up her pen and began to write.

Chapter 16

"It's your lucky day Nurse Merrigan," Nurse Slater called out. She was swinging the keys and making her way to the stores where a fresh consignment of goods had just been delivered. "Coach trip for you today."

The radio had been switched off and the tv turned on in readiness for Crown Court. All the remaining patients had been settled and warned that the staff wanted absolute peace and quiet.

The maroon and cream coach swung into view. There was a buzz of excitement amongst the lucky patients who had been selected for today's trip. They had crowded in the foyer waiting for the first glimpse of Ken, and to hear the traditional two beeps of the horn.

Mary was rushing to the door and in her haste, did not see Nurse Slater put out her foot to trip her up.

"Who said you could go, Ryan?"

"Oh, let her go Jean. We don't want her whining all the way through our programme. It will put me off my chocolate!".

"Go on then. Get up. You heard Sister. Stupid, clumsy cow."

Already forgotten, Nurse Slater slipped off her shoes and tucked her legs beneath her, while popping a square of a chocolate bar in her mouth. Dairy Milk, Shelley thought. Sister Berry shifted Lily out of her chair to get the best view of the telly.

"Are you okay, Mary?" Shelley asked as they made their way to the coach.

"Okay," Mary echoed. Shelley was not sure if she was just parroting her or whether she was seeking to reassure the young nurse. Shelley patted her hand. Mary drew her hand back abruptly and Shelley understood how hyper vigilant to attack these women were.

"I'm sorry," she said uselessly.

Lara was not on the coach. She had not been allowed back on since the incident when she had had to be restrained. Ken had said he was willing to give it another go, maybe with more staff, he had suggested tentatively. It was a blanket "no" from the ward sister. He was tenderhearted and had been shaken by the incident. He had told his wife when he got home that evening. She had listened patiently and poured him a little of his favourite whiskey.

"Only half an inch mind, Sheila. You don't want me lagging and sentimental."

Shelley was the last one on the coach. Ken gave her a big smile as she got on. He really was one of life's rare gems. "Got the short straw?" he laughed, as he handed her a Kia Ora carton and a scone wrapped in foil. "If you don't want it, you can lob it out of the window. The seagulls can sharpen their beaks on it," he joked. It was actually delicious and gave Shelley a stab of homesickness.

Shelley's mood lightened as the coach maneuvered out of the hospital gates. She realised with a jolt that she hadn't been out of the grounds since last payday when her and Julie went for a Chinese take away through the back gate of the hospital. A month tomorrow. It seemed it was just as easy for the staff to become institutionalised. Everything you needed was right here. Work, home, canteen, social club. There was even a mini launderette.

"Well good afternoon, ladies," Ken said. "Relax and enjoy the view as we go on a magical mystery tour."

Smiling into his rear-view mirror, he turned on the radio.

"Let me know if you have any requests ladies," he said as he sang along to Glen Campbell's *Rhinestone Cowboy*. Shelley looked at the patients. They looked more at ease than she had seen them before. Rosanna Hope from Ivy ward was smiling and humming along. Lesley Muller had stopped biting her hand. And Mary had stopped looking pensive and had the faintest hint of a smile as she looked out of the window at the shifting landscape. They could have been any group out for a little jaunt, Shelley thought, recalling the annual Sunday school outing to Brittas Bay, and the end of her crush on Brendan Kelly as she saw him vomit the contents of his Shippams Fish Paste sandwich into an empty crisp packet.

Deep in thought, Shelley sat up quickly when Ken said they were nearly at their destination. They went through a village with regulation pub, The Rose, a church, post office and fish and chip shop. Landscove Parish Church, Shelley read on the board outside the church in a well-tended graveyard. There were tea rooms set back from the road that looked like they had once been a guide hall, boasting the best cream teas in Cornwall.

"Not a patch on my Sheila's scones though eh?" Ken said as he took a sharp turn down a narrow lane with high hedges either side.

"Breathe in ladies," Ken smiled, as he skillfully negotiated the bends and turns in the lane.

The lane widened and then Ken announced, "Here we are," as he swung onto a gravelled path between two imposing grey stone gateposts. Under a green sign saying THE NATIONAL TRUST was the name of the house. Celyn Lodge.

"Now, I have spoken to an old friend of mine, Joff, who just happens to be the head gardener here. He has given us permission to park in front of the house so we can all have a good old nosey. Proper 'ansom this place is," he said.

Grinding slowly over the gravel, Ken came to a stop outside Celyn.

"Here he is," Ken said, as a man in his late fifties approached the coach. The men shook hands warmly and Joff doffed his cap at the ladies. The patients didn't leave the coach, so Shelley enjoyed the spectacle of the house from her seat. It was beautiful, perfectly symmetrical with grey stones with some purple flower Shelley did not know the name of. Everything about the house was gratifying. She could see what she thought was a body of water glistening across the manicured lawns. There was a wooded area to the side and curved around the house was what looked like a path leading off away from the house.

Interrupting her thoughts, Rosanna called out "Nurse". She needed the toilet. Shelley looked to her fellow escort, a nursing assistant she had not met before for some direction as to what to do.

"Well, you can take her or let her piss in her pants. Your call," she said.

Shelley looked at Ken.

"I won't say anything if you don't," he said, so Shelley led her off the bus to where Joff had indicated the toilets were located.

Shelley went through the magnificent wooden double doors and across the parquet flooring to the ladies. As she ushered a relieved Rosanna back towards the coach, she plucked a leaflet about Celyn Lodge from the wire display stand and stuffed it deep into her uniform pocket. She would love to return one day and have a leisurely look around. Ken had told her the path she had seen led down to a private cove. She wondered if Julie would go with her but swiftly dismissed the idea. It wouldn't be her scene, but she wondered if she knew anything about Celyn Lodge, being a Cornish native and all that. She would check the off duty and see if there was a bus to Landscove from Mallock.

The journey back to Wellswood seemed quicker than the way there and soon Shelley was soon shepherding the patients off the coach. The carefree atmosphere evaporated on the last step of the coach with Ken's cheery goodbyes.

Shelley followed the patients as they wandered back into Cypress and the others scurried off to their wards. What a contrast. The smell that Shelley had become used to hit her afresh as she opened the doors and entered the dayroom. She saw tea was already in progress as she slipped off her coat and hung it in the office. Remembering the leaflet, she took it out of her dress and pushed it deep into her coat pocket. She did not want it discovered that she had left the coach.

Nurse Slater was doing the drug round. She seemed cheerful as she dispensed the medication.

"Two blue ones and three yellows for Henty," she almost sang.

The medicine trolley was attached to the wall by a chain when not in use in the clinic room. It was made from teak, Shelley guessed. The top part opened like a piano lid. There was a small bar to keep the prescription charts in place, a little like a music stand. Unless Mr. Scott was doing his rounds, it was redundant, as Nurse Slater and Sister Berry never consulted the drug charts, seeming to know the medication and who had what by heart.

"Lady Muck has buggered off before getting her meds. Take these down to Lara." She handed Shelley a small plastic pot containing two large white tablets. She went to the kitchen to get some water. Janet, the ward domestic was washing up in the large sink where billows of steam were filling the kitchen. Hard of hearing, she did not hear Shelley come in. She jumped in alarm when Shelley came beside her to get water. The front of Janet's orange overall uniform was soaked. There was some vigorous dishwashing going on Shelley thought. Janet stared intently at the water and carried on scrubbing at plates. Shelley could see she had been crying. Her eyes were red, and she wiped her nose with the back of her suds-soaked hands.

"Oh, now, Janet" said Shelley softly. "What have we here?" emulating the gentle tones of her Ma when in a soothing mood.

Janet looked at her and looked about to say something when Nurse Slater burst through the door. She plunged her hands back into the scalding water.

"I thought I told you to take Lara her tablets".

"Yes, yes, you did. I was just getting some water".

"This lot don't need water. None of them need water with their tablets. Just do as you are told," she said, exasperated. Without argument, or water, Shelley wandered down the dormitory to Lara's side room. She knocked on the door before gently opening it. She smiled and greeted Lara with a cheerfulness she did not feel. She wondered what had caused Nurse Slater's cheeriness and Janet's tears, knowing the two events were likely to be related.

Apologetically, she handed Lara the two large tablets into her cupped hands. Lara threw them to the back of her throat and gulped loudly. Nurse Slater was right. No water required. She struggled to find something to say. Oh yes, Dr Winstanley advised her to give a running commentary. Talk naturally about your day. She remembered in time that Lara had become very disturbed during her last and final coach trip, so she avoided that subject. With some relief, she remembered tomorrow's session with Dr Winstanley and was pleased to have something meaningful to say.

"Well goodnight Lara. I will see you tomorrow."

As she walked back to her room after her shift, she resolved to try and speak to Janet. She might be an ally. Shelley had not taken much notice of her before. Nurse Slater had told her Janet was as deaf as a post, so there was no point in talking to her. She was small and wiry and was like a clockwork toy, Shelley thought: the only time she stopped was to go out of the back kitchen for a smoke. She even smoked quickly, drawing deeply and intensely on her Silk Cut purples. She was married. Shelley had seen the thin gold band she wore on her permanently detergent-reddened hands. Her husband was the porter who delivered the big silver dinner trolleys up from the kitchens.

Chapter 17

That night, Shelley was so tired she fell asleep on top of the covers, still in her uniform. She woke with a start and rolled over to check the time on her clock radio. 03.27 a.m. Oh, my living stars, the giant penny dropped. How could she have missed this? She staggered over towards the door and fumbled for the light switch. Adjusting her eyes to the light, she found what she was looking for. Retrieving the crumpled leaflet from her coat pocket, she smoothed it out to look at the name on the top. Celyn Lodge. She had seen that name before. Lara's notes. It was where Lara was taken on that coach trip when she had inexplicably erupted with rage and had tried to get off the coach. She was sure she had the name right. She was on duty at 7 a.m. so only a few hours until she could check. But why on earth would Lara become agitated at a National Trust property? It made little sense. The questions churned until she fell asleep at 6.20 a.m., ten minutes before her alarm went off.

The clock radio crackled into life with the dulcet tones of Dolly Parton singing *Jolene, Jolene*. Shelley groaned and considered the day ahead. Remembering her mission energized her. She got dressed quickly and made her way to Cypress. She could feel the change of season in the air; it was getting lighter earlier, and spring was on the way. She turned the name over in her mind. Celyn Lodge. Shelley knew she would not be able to look at the notes until the morning duties were completed. Dr Winstanley was due to visit Lara again at 11 a.m.; she hoped to be able to cross reference the name of Celyn to the case notes entry before she arrived on the ward. Shelley had secreted the leaflet in her dress pocket to show the Doctor if she was right.

It was a particularly busy morning which meant the time passed quickly and before long Shelley heard Dr Winstanley and Sister Berry talking in the foyer. Her little mouth puckering in distaste, Sister called Shelley to let her know she could be relieved from her duties until lunchtime.

"Will I fetch the notes?" asked Shelley. She hoped she would have enough time to scan them before Dr Winstanley summoned Lara so she could show her what she had discovered.

"Yes, yes," she replied absently, taking off her coat and uncoiling her scarf. She had evidently just extinguished a cigarette as the smell of tobacco was pervasive.

Shelley retrieved the notes from the filing cabinet. She sifted through them trying to find the entry she was looking for. There it was! Student Nurse Angela Blackledge's careful entry for August 10th, 1972.

Tracing the notes with her finger, she scrutinized the words. She was correct. Lara had become seriously agitated at Celyn Lodge. She double checked the leaflet again, wanting to be sure before she presented her findings to Dr Winstanley. Certain now, she went into the quiet room.

"I don't know what to make of this," Shelley said, spreading out the leaflet and indicating the case notes. The doctor read the notes and picked up the leaflet.

"A National Trust property? Celyn Lodge?" It dawned on them both that there was no home address for Lara in her notes. Dr Winstanley wondered if Lara had been raised near Landscove and was aware of the house. What, if any, was the significance of Lara's outburst and Celyn Lodge.

Dr Winstanley was aware there were supplementary notes archived in the large administrative block in the front of the hospital. She wondered if she might find out more if she delved into the archived material. There might be a home address and more information about the circumstances surrounding her admission than were contained in the ward's notes.

"Hmm," was all the Doctor said before asking Shelley to fetch Lara. Lara slipped into her seat opposite Dr Winstanley. Much more neutral today, she no longer looked at Shelley with suspicion. Today, she accepted the offer of a cup of tea and stuffed the chocolate chip cookie into her mouth with some speed. Dr Winstanley stifled a smile and pretended not to take any notice of her acceptance of refreshments. Progress, she thought to herself.

"Shall we try something else this week Lara." This was not couched as a question. "I have brought a few things for you. I wondered if you would like to have a look in this bag."

She handed the bag over to Lara who looked at it dully.

"Take a peek," urged the doctor.

First Lara pulled out a tiny, knitted cardigan in a lemon yellow. Lara looked at the cardigan and then at the doctor. She ran her hand across the knotted material and stroked the shiny little buttons.

"Carry on, there's more."

She knew this was a risky strategy and it could either go horribly wrong or nudge Lara towards a breakthrough. But she had a hunch and was willing to trust her instincts and go for it.

Next, she pulled out a tiny pink dummy with a little ribbon attached to the handle. Lara looked at both objects with a look of bewilderment and anticipation.

"There's more."

Lara rooted around in the bag and pulled out a large pink box with butterflies on. "Tiny Tears," said the label.

"Would you like me to open it?" enquired the doctor. For the longest time, Lara stared at the unopened box. The doctor worried she had made an error of judgement, gone too fast, blown it, but then Lara gave the first indication in decades that she was not an empty vessel. She nodded.

Hiding her amazement, Dr Winstanley opened the box and sought to free the little doll from the plastic bindings that tethered her to the box. She handed the doll to Lara, who lifted it to her nose and inhaled deeply. Picking up the cardigan, she unbuttoned it and gently dressed the little doll. She popped the dummy in her mouth, seemed to decide against it, and slipped the dummy in her own dress pocket.

"One more thing in the bag, Lara," she said, pulling out a matching knitted hat, silently thanking the women from the League of Friends who were fervent knitters. Lara took the hat and placed it on the doll's head, adjusting it until she was satisfied it was in the correct position snugly covering its ears. Lara liked the way the doll closed her eyes as she tipped her into a sleeping position. She liked her blonde hair and the way she smelled. Suddenly conscious of her audience, Lara placed the doll on the small table that separated her from the doctor.

"She's for you Lara. All yours. If you want her."

She hesitated.

"I won't let them take her," she said, intuitively sensing this was the cause of her restraint.

Lara picked up the doll and cradled it to her chest. She buttoned her cardigan over the baby and stood up.

"It was good to see you again, Lara. Thank you for coming. I will see you again on Tuesday if that is okay." Lara lingered at the shut door momentarily. She then opened it and hurried off to her room to have some alone time with her very own baby girl.

The two women looked at each other aghast. "Well, that answers a whole buncha questions Shelley!" Dr Winstanley said.

"My case study has just taken a whole new turn!"

"Keep this on the down low Shelley. Lara will keep that doll quiet and so must you. Don't let the bitches piss on her chips." Shelley already knew this would be a secret between her and Lara. What she did not know at that point was they would share a far bigger secret very soon that both of them would take to their graves.

Chapter 18

The following Monday after ward round, Dr Winstanley made her way to the administrative building of the hospital. The façade was imposing and attractive with large sash windows. It housed all the heads of department offices and the hospital records. Extinguishing her cigarette on the stone steps leading to the entrance, she called out to Helen who operated the front reception desk.

"Ah, good morning, Doctor. I will be with you in two ticks," she said, as she pulled a sheet of paper deftly out of the typewriter. "Can I leave you to it?" she asked, handing the keys to the doctor, who nodded, smiled and held her hands out to receive them.

She walked down the corridor to the door behind which contained all the case records since Wellswood first opened its doors. Dr Winstanley always felt she was entering the very bowels of the hospital as she descended the stone stairs to the rows of shelves that contained the yellowing histories of those who lived and died here. It smelled of damp and mice and she shivered despite the warmth of the day outside. She went down the D-F aisle. Davies, Davenport, Demengel, Lara. Found it. It wasn't the tome she had been hoping for, but it was something at least. She returned the keys to

Helen and gave a parting wave as Helen was on the phone.

She hurried along the path that led to her office on Cherry. Silently she prayed she would not be intercepted on the way so she could settle down and read Lara's notes. She quickly made herself a coffee, strong and black. She opened her window the few inches it would, to let the fumes out when she smoked.

She opened the notes. An easy win. On the first page was a letter from a Dr Franklin. With his address.

3 Fore Street

Landscove.

If he was from Landscove and attended Lara's family, she must have lived close by. She continued to read and then abruptly grabbed her jacket and rushed to Cypress, hoping Shelley was on duty. Horribly out of breath, she arrived at Cypress. Composing herself, she entered the dayroom. Nurse Slater swiveled around in surprise and in a seamless movement, snapped shut the medicine trolley she had been rummaging around in; selecting a sedative for Olivia who had been laying on the ground shaking her head and refusing to get up.

"What can I do you for, Doctor?" she asked as she recovered herself.

"I am looking for Nurse Merrigan," Doctor Winstanley replied.

"Join the club. We are always looking for her when there is any work to be done," she laughed to dilute her toxic comment.

Shelley appeared from the direction of the bathrooms leading a freshly bathed Eva back to her chair.

Wordlessly, she inclined her head towards the office and Shelley followed, intrigued by her unscheduled visit and disheveled appearance.

"When's your next day off?" she asked. "You and I are going on a little outing!".

Chapter 19

Shelley woke up early on the Thursday, her day off. She went down the corridor to the shower room. Happily, there was no queue for the bathroom today. The bathroom was stark and utilitarian. She did not like to linger; the shower curtain was thin and permanently damp and chill, flapping against her cold body while a lame flow of scalding water left her with the red rivulets she noticed as she dried herself with the towel her Ma had bought from Cleary's.

"You'll not be showing us up with a thin towel!" Ma had said, folding it onto the top of her clothes in her suitcase. Shelley smiled at the memory as she looked in her drawers for something to wear. 06.30. The clock radio snapped into life and Shelley sang along to *The way we were*. She recalled saying to her Ma she wished she had the kind of voice that made people cry.

"You have, Shelley," she replied with a straight face, thereby putting an end to her dreams of being the next Shirley Bassey.

She gave her skirt a shake. It needed an iron, but Shelley hoped the creases might drop out as the day wore on. It was a blue and white peasant skirt with an uneven hem. She stretched a white top over her large chest, wishing she wasn't so cumbersome. She tried to adjust the top so her wide bra strap, which cut a deep groove into her shoulders, wasn't on view. Thank goodness, she thought, for her lustrous hair which fell past her shoulders, thick and dark brown. God had to give her something to compensate for having the build of a navvy she thought.

She felt nervous as she waited for Dr Winstanley outside Bawtree House. She was way too early.

"Morning Nurse," said the man she had met on her first day who had been struggling with the big trolley. Shelley had thought he was grimacing with the effort of pushing, but now realised he had cerebral palsy and his face was in perpetual motion. "Got a fag?" he chanced. Apologetically she shook her head. She watched as he scoured the ground for dog ends to create a roll-up for himself.

A red MG roadster, roof down, skidded up alongside her.

"Get in Shelley," Dr Winstanley said without any preamble.

Shelley slumped down heavily into the bucket seat, already worried about how she would extricate herself at the end of her journey. She was embarrassed as she felt she was encroaching over the gear stick with her thighs. She tried to shift herself as far towards the passenger door as possible.

The doctor was a conundrum. Shelley had expected a Citroen Diane maybe or something less racy. Dr Winstanley pushed the lighter in and plucked herself a cigarette from the pack. She offered the packet to Shelley, who declined, and tossed the pack onto the dashboard.

"Dr Winstanley?" Shelley ventured.

"Today, you must call me Vix. It's short for Victoria but all my friends call me Vix." Vix seemed much younger than Dr Winstanley. She had sunglasses on against the glare of the early summer sun that was making an effort to heat the day. She was wearing a denim shirt tied at the waist and what looked like good quality white linen capri trousers. Her hair hung loose down her back. "Oh, she's attractive. For her age obviously," Shelley realised for the first time.

"There is a map in the glove compartment. But my husband has written down some directions for us. Here." She shoved a scrap of paper into her lap. Landscove was twenty two miles away. Vix turned on the radio and Shelley had to keep reminding herself this was business and not a jolly. She was glad of the map, not confident that she could retrace the route taken by Ken in the coach just last week.

Shelley had not yet seen the supplementary notes found by Dr Winstanley. It was more astounding than either of them had expected; Lara's family had actually lived in Celyn Lodge until it was taken over by the National Trust. They speculated that perhaps she had a connection to the village of Landscove following the revelation about Dr Franklin's address. But that she had been raised in the most prestigious house in the region was totally unexpected. Celyn Lodge had been taken over by the Trust in 1952 in a post war collaboration between the national land fund and the horticultural society. But what had happened to the Demengel family? Was there anyone left who could provide some answers? Dr Franklin had written in his letter that he had been the family physician for a long time and had known Lara since infancy. He would be an incredibly old man if he was still alive. They were going to try and find Fore Street after visiting Celyn Lodge.

Smoothing the map across her lap, Shelley told Vix to turn left at the next junction. Before them in the distance was a sliver of aquamarine beyond the patchwork of green fields. Shelley marvelled at the colour of the ocean in Cornwall; it looked Mediterranean. The lane narrowed and the car was flanked by high hedgerows that obstructed the view.

"Pretty much a straight road for the next few miles, Vix." It sounded alien to her to call her Vix and not Dr Winstanley and she felt awkward, so tried to avoid calling her anything.

Shelley allowed herself to sit back in the seat and enjoy the feeling of the wind whipping up her hair. The car was noisy, and she would rather have had the radio off. It whined and competed with the engine and the wind. As if reading her mind, Vix turned the radio off and reached across for her cigarettes. She did not bother offering Shelley one this time. Both women retreated into the reverie of their own thoughts. The only break in the quiet was Shelley issuing directions.

"Oh here, here," Shelley said, as Vix almost drove past the gateposts that stood like sentries at the entrance to Celyn Lodge. She swerved the car in, and they crunched over the gravel drive towards the house. They funnelled down the drive in between the cordons festooned with bunting and arrows pointing to the car park. Shelley clambered out of the car with less grace than she would have liked and stretched her legs. Vix leapt out and yawned. She scooped up her cigarettes and put them into her small handbag. She perched her sunglasses on her head.

"Let's go," she said.

They followed the gravelled paths that snaked in between immaculate lawns and flower beds. And then, rising before them, was the grandeur and beauty of Celyn Lodge itself.

"Wow, that is a cracker of a pad," whistled Dr Winstanley. "Look at all that wisteria; it looks like it's been decorated especially for us!"

They bought their tickets, confirming they wanted to have a tour of the house and visit the gardens and the private cove. Dr Winstanley bought the map and tour guide pamphlet and quickly scanned its pages for any mention of the Demengels. The only mention was that the property had been purchased in 1952 and had previously been owned by the Demengel family. That was it. No other information. The girl on reception looked about twenty so she would not have known the family, but Dr Winstanley thought she might chance her arm.

The young girl looked up cheerily when Dr Winstanley returned to the ticket desk and asked if there was any more information about the family. She apologized and said she did not know anything about them. She was not local and was just doing a little stint in the house as part of her tourism course at Redruth College. As the Doctor walked away, she mentioned that the old gardener had been here for years and apparently had worked for the Demengels since he was a young man. Shelley remembered he was a friend of Ken's. She had seen him on the previous visit. Jeff or something?

"We will have a quick gander around the house and then let's look out for our gardener."

The house was magnificent. It smelled of polished wood with lemony undertones, Shelley thought. It had huge, grand, fireplaces and deep window seats, just made for reading on a rainy day. It was impossible to reconcile that Lara Demengel had once lived here, with all its grace and splendour with the contrast of Cypress villa, stark, clinical and terrifying. Shelley wondered where she had slept, played, ate. The tour took in the vast downstairs kitchen, the engine room of the house, unaware that this had been Lara's favourite place before her exile to Nancy's cottage.

"I can't feel her here somehow." Shelley said.

The doctor agreed. There was no trace of Lara, nothing to connect her to this building.

"Let us find Jeff."

They blinked in the bright sunlight as they left the cool of the house. The day was warming up and the sun was high. There was no sign of the older man, so the doctor strode towards a young man in dungarees pruning a rose bush.

"Hi there. I am looking for Jeff?" the doctor asked.

He looked momentarily puzzled. "Oh, you mean Joff? He's working at the pond. Just over there," he said, and pointed.

They walked towards where he had pointed. Shining in the sun light was the pond which was wide and deep; the river had been diverted to create a pool. Joff was pulling some reeds from the edge of the pond and loading them onto his wheelbarrow. The water had breached his waders and his trousers were wet. When he heard Dr Winstanley call his name he looked up, shielding his eyes from the glare of the sun. He did not recognise the women, but stopped his work and walked towards them, curious now as to how they knew his name.

"Hello. Can I help you ladies?"

"We are hopeful that you can. Apparently, you have worked here for a long time. Before the National Trust took it over? When the Demengel family were still here?"

"Ah. I see. Not sure how good the old memory is! But true enough I have been here since I were knee high."

His manner was jovial as he plucked a tin of rolling tobacco from his shirt pocket.

"Fire away Miss, and I'll see if I can help you.".

"Do you know anything about a Lara Demengel?"

Barely perceptible to the untrained eye, Joff hesitated as he went to lick his Rizla, a blush crept up his neck. He looked up to the middle distance as if he were trying to remember something. Conversely, he had been trying to forget Lara and what he had done for the past forty years.

"Nope. Sorry lover. Said my memory wasn't what it was. Terrible with names." He turned his back on them and resumed his work.

The women turned away, disappointed. They decided to take the path down to the beach. They picked up a path that led away from the house and through a wooded area. The sun dappled through the boughs of the trees creating shafts of light on the beach trail. The path gave way to small dunes and then before them lay the crescent cove. Dr Winstanley kicked off her sandals. The sand was cold and wet; the tide must be going out.

The waves rolled in in a mesmerising rhythm, dumping heavily on the shoreline and retreating with a strenuous backwash.

"I wonder if she came down here," she pondered, almost to herself, forgetting she was not alone. She lit another cigarette, as if the questions might be answered by a Marlboro Light.

They both gazed at the horizon, lost in their individual thoughts, but with one common theme. Lara.

Shelley was hungry. She did not want to mention it in case the doctor judged her appetite to be grotesque in some way. She suspected the doctor's thinness was achieved by heavy smoking, black coffee, and a degree of agitation.

"I think I spotted a little place selling ice cream and coffees on the way in. Fancy one before we head into town?" Shelley answered in a measured way that gave off an air of being casual and agreed it would be tolerable.

They made their way back to the car. They both felt deflated, having nurtured some optimism about gleaning some answers today.

"I will just pull in. What do you fancy?" Shelley would have loved a double deluxe ice cream with a flake and maybe topped with a globule of clotted cream but asked for a single cone of vanilla. There were two white plastic tables and four chairs outside. There was a stable door leading to the kitchen service area where a quaint old-fashioned range, blackened and decorative, with an old brass kettle for display could be seen. By an old, scrubbed pine dresser, there was a small display of books for sale. "Traditional Cornish Bakes" caught Dr Winstanley's eye. She had been drawn to the front cover with a mouthwatering picture of a scone with jam and clotted cream. She ferreted around the bottom of her bag to find her purse to pay. She handed the ice cream to Shelley and flicked through the glossy pictures.

"I don't know why I buy these. I never cook," she laughed. "But I like to imagine one day I will don a frilly apron and get baking before hubby comes home," she giggled at the thought. "He does all the cooking in ours. The husband I mean."

"Hmm. What a great name for a cook. Look, Cooke. Inspired by recipes by Nancy Cooke. Bung this by your feet, will you please," as she drove towards the exit and then towards Landscove.

Fore Street was the main street through Landscove. Number Four was now the fish and chip shop which was open for lunchtime trade. A spotty lad sweating into his chef's whites shook his head when asked if he knew anything about a Dr Franklin. He carried on rotating the chips with a mini shovel; he did not know of anyone who could help either.

"I don't know about you, but I need a coffee. I saw a tea shop. I am hoping they do coffee too!"

They walked down the street and into the tea shop. "Ye Olde Tea Shoppe," the menu stated.

"Take a seat and I'll come and take your order," a smiling waitress with receding gums and a tight ponytail said.

"Oh, you have to order food between 12 and 2pm," the doctor said. "Do you want anything?" Saying a silent prayer of thanks, Shelley said she thought she might be able to manage a pasty and beans.

While they were waiting for their food and drinks to arrive, Shelley got out the guide map for Celyn to check over it again to see if they had missed anything. The waitress came with a small tray and started to lay out their drinks, little cartons of milk, and sachets of sugar.

"Oh, been to Celyn Lodge, have you? Nice day for it. Pretty this time of year, isn't it? Can I get you anything else before your food arrives? Hot water for your coffee? My Mum talks about Celyn all the time, especially now she is losing her mind poor girl. She was in service there for years. Tragic what happened to them Demengels. See, money don't buy happiness as they say. Wouldn't mind giving it a go though!" she said, chuckling at her own little joke and heading back towards the kitchen.

"Your Mum. She's still alive? And she worked at Celyn Lodge?" the doctor asked.

Turning back to look at Dr Winstanley, she said she was indeed, although was frail and dementing since having a mini stroke 18 months ago.

"She has had to move in with me, Brian and the kids. Dad passed 20 years ago, and Mum had been independent until the stroke. She kept falling and had started up with these delusions. Confabulating, the doctor called it. Her lives in the past, she does. Keeps going down memory lane and talking nonsense."

"Could I talk to her?" the doctor interrupted. The waitress looked aghast. "I am sorry. I should explain. I haven't even asked your name!"

Unsure of the enthusiasm of this stranger, she reservedly said her name. Louise Gidley. That's my married name. I was Newby. My mother's name is Cally. Cally Newby.

Chapter 20

The next morning, Shelley and Dr Winstanley woke up in the upstairs guest room of "The Rose" in Landscove. They had decided to stay the night after persuading Louise to talk to her mother.

"She is better in the morning," Louise had said. "Hopeless in the afternoon, mind. She just sleeps and talks rubbish when she is awake."

It was Louise who had suggested staying over at The Rose. It had upped its game from the spit and sawdust reputation of yesteryear, replacing bare knuckle fights with velour banquette seating and flocked wallpaper. Shelley was exhausted and needed sleep desperately after three large glasses of dry white wine in the lounge bar the night before. They did a reasonable breakfast too. It was the barman from last night who served them their fry up. Both women had felt giggly the night before as they talked about the ludicrously handsome young man with Hollywood looks. He had glossy black hair and almost navy eyes. He negotiated his way in between the tables with a dancer's grace. He made Shelley feel like an East German discus thrower. They looked at each other and smiled as he waited on them, remembering their slightly drunken musings about him the night before.

"And me, an old married woman! He has made me feel alive again!" Doctor Winstanley exclaimed.

Replete, they followed Louise's directions to her house which was a short walk from Fore Street. Louise answered the door. Two teenage boys, Louise's sons, Shelley presumed, fought to get out of the front door, each clutching a quarter of a slice of toast and grunting a farewell to their mother.

"Oh, I have one of those at home!" the doctor said, forming an invisible bond with Louise.

"She's in here," she said, and led them into the front room. Despite the warmth of the day, there was an open fire already dancing in the hearth. "Sorry, Mum feels the cold. Even in August she wants the fire lit."

Cally was listing in a high, wing backed chair. Left sided weakness assessed the doctor. There was a slight tug to her mouth and her eyes were closed with a half-drunk cup of tea perilously close to spilling down her pink quilted bed jacket. Shelley's heart lurched in her chest with a clear memory of her Nanna wearing the same universal housebound old lady uniform and felt a pang of homesickness.

"Mum," she called her again, slightly louder. Her mum woke with a start and Louise reassured her with a hand on her arm and the smile that showed off her gums. "Mum, we have guests," she said. Cally looked around until her eyes fixed on Shelley and Dr Winstanley. The doctor knelt before her to establish eye contact and modulated her voice whilst introducing herself and Shelley, who stood awkwardly near the door. Cally looked at them through the opaque lens of cataracts. Dr Winstanley said she wanted to talk to her because she understood Cally had worked at Celyn Lodge and they were keen to hear any memories she may have about the family. The Demengels? She further prompted. Cally closed her eyes and took a deep breath.

"Shot himself." she said.

"Who, Cally? Who shot himself?"

"Oh, poor Nancy. My best friend ever was."

Her speech was indistinct, but the doctor had worked with enough dysphasic patients to pick up Cally's speech patterns.

"Killed her, she did. "

"Oh, here she goes again," lamented Louise. "Off on one. I know she had a best friend called Nancy who was the cook at Celyn who passed away. She told me that when I was young, and she took me to see her grave in the churchyard and she put flowers on it regular. A special big bunch in October. Mum used to get all choked up and said she didn't want to talk about it. Well, she is making up for it now! She didn't really like to talk about her but now it is all she goes on about. Says she was killed. Rambles on about the evil one. I thought she was talking about the devil, but she said the devil had a name. I asked her who, who is the evil one? I had known the names of the family, those dead and those still alive as I had grown up hearing the names and later, reading the headstones in the churchyard. The Demengel children. Theo, Bertie, Emmeline and Milla. Mum gets so agitated about her. The Doctor said she is probably delusional, part of her condition. But it is a persistent one! She repeats the name over and over. Lara, Lara, Lara.

PART 3

Chapter 21

30th October 1937

Dr Franklin, Tabitha Hollis, Cally and Loveday congregated together around the bloodied pile of sheets still warm after Lara had been torn from them, kicking and screaming.

"It's for the best, Loveday," Dr Franklin said. She did not need convincing. She had already made up her mind that this was to be kept from Charles and from the rest of her family. She just had to make sure that she could rely on discretion from those in the room, who had now become her co-conspirators. She looked at the sleeping baby, blissfully unaware she had just been torn from her mother forever. Impassively, Loveday regarded her granddaughter. All she could see was shame and a dilemma. She cursed Lara for bringing her nothing but grief. Weren't children supposed to be a blessing?

"What can be done with the child?" She wished that she could be bundled up with the sheets, incinerated and duly forgotten. She did not want her life tainted in this way. She had the other children to think about; their prospects and standing in Landscove (and beyond) in tatters if this story was to haemorrhage beyond these walls. She knew enough of Cally to know she could pay for her silence. Dr Franklin naturally would be discreet;

he had taken the oath. But Tabitha? She had never even heard of her.

She addressed her now. "Would you and Cally deal with this bloodbath? I need to speak with Dr Franklin."

Darkness was falling as they went outside the stable door to talk in private. Dr Franklin vouched for Tabitha Hollis, saying she was the soul of discretion. With her anxiety abating slightly, she returned to the little room where the infant was beginning to stir. Tabitha looked at the child. Almost without any premeditation, she knew what she was going to do.

"Miss?" she ventured. "I can take the child. Till you figure out what to do? I can say my sister has taken ill after giving birth. She lives a way off and I have a houseful already."

Embarrassed, she looked down and said milk wouldn't be a problem; she was still nursing her youngest.

Loveday would have given the child to a passing peddler, so agreed without hesitation and within moments, Tabitha had wrapped the baby in clean towels and a cardigan from Nancy's cupboards and was driven by Dr Franklin to her home in the village.

Now there was just the issue of Cally to contend with. With sudden inspiration, she offered Nancy's cottage to her and her husband, Ted Newby. They were childless. Loveday had never even considered how old Cally was. She seemed to have been at Celyn for years. She had moved out of Celyn's service quarters when she had met and married Ted at the age of eighteen, by which time she had already been employed for three years. She was now twenty-five. Nancy's cottage would be an upgrade for sure. They lived in a single room in

Ted's mother's house. Gratefully, Cally seized on the opportunity whilst offering up a prayer of apology to Nancy for jumping in when she was barely cold.

"You understand, Cally, that tonight's events must, of course, remain secret. I will reward you handsomely, you and your husband. But if you ever breach my confidence, you will have to leave. You will lose your job and your home. Are we clear?"

Cally nodded her agreement despite her desperation to run to Celyn and tell everyone she met. She adored a morsel of gossip to chew around but promised her allegiance to Loveday. She reckoned she would just have to think of the prospect of returning to live with Ted's mother criticizing her every move to motivate her to keep quiet if ever the desire to gossip overtook her. It seemed a small price to pay. The cottage and a payoff. All she had to do was keep quiet. She was sure even she could do it. The deal was done.

Chapter 22

Dolly Hollis was a darling baby, loved by all of Tabitha's older children. Even Ross Hollis was won over. She became the centre of their universe. She was a much prettier baby than Tabitha's own, who were large, sturdy types who looked like farmhands from infancy, even the girls. Dolly was petite and delicate looking, not fussy and laughed easily at the older children. Tabitha had developed a deep-seated dread that Dolly would be taken from her, if a more permanent solution was found. But still the money kept rolling in for her upkeep. Dr Franklin came every month to hand it over personally. He did not linger and never looked at the child; she was a bastard and a problem as far as he was concerned. By the time Dolly was three, Tabitha had relaxed and realised that indeed, she was the permanent solution. She never had a moment's regret. Even without the money, they would have kept her. Dolly had them all enthralled with her fairy like ways and sweet nature.

The villagers accepted the story that Tabitha's sister had died from complications of childbirth. It happened so frequently as not to raise any suspicions and Tabitha had so many siblings herself, she could be vague about the details. War had broken out and people became consumed with other, more pressing matters. Dolly's life played out like every other child's in the village, untainted by the war. They still played outdoors in the fields until sundown and often they all headed down to the beach. The older Hollis children never resented Dolly tagging along. Nobody could really remember a time before she came and graced their lives. Tabitha concealed her worries about food scarcity from the children. She proved herself a mistress of stealth, scouring farmland for a cabbage here, potatoes there. The children were tucked up safely in their beds whilst Tabitha prayed on the stairs for their safekeeping and forgiveness for foraging in Hilltop Farms fields. Ross would hold his wife close and kiss the top of her forehead as he counted his blessings for his little family, and their distance from London at this time.

Celyn Lodge 3rd September 1939. Sunday.

Loveday and Milla prepared carefully for church. Sundays were always a good day to showcase her daughters. Emmeline was still in bed, having had a little too much to drink at a party in Chelston Manor the night before. She also wanted to swerve her mother's relentless questioning about the progress of her courtship with Ernest Blackledge, a perennial bore. She wanted to avoid her beady eyes alighting on her neck, where she was sporting a love bite from the very handsome valet who had helped her find her way back to the ballroom from the ladies' room.

Charles Demengel was in his study. He had been increasingly agitated for the past few weeks as the rumours of the war had intensified. He only barely tolerated Chivers around him these days; Chivers was used to him and seemed impervious to his truculence and erratic moods. He had already barked at Chivers to leave him alone this morning. He poured himself a large whiskey, which he rolled around in the crystal glass before knocking it back in a single movement. He poured himself another. The front door slammed shut behind his wife and daughter leaving for church. Charles jolted in alarm. He began to sweat and shake as he hung on to the glass for dear life. He gripped his desk to steady himself. As the shaking abated, he began to cry.

At 11.10, he turned on the radio to listen to the expected announcement by Neville Chamberlain. He turned the dial until the crackling stopped and the clear tones of the home service reverberated against the wood panelling of the study. He sat in his green leather chair by the fire and listened with the whole of Britain to the voice of Neville Chamberlain announcing:

"The country is at war with Germany."

The tremors and tears stopped.

Charles drained his whiskey and walked to his desk, which was walnut with a red leather top, and opened the drawer. He rummaged around under estate paperwork until he found what he needed. His WW1 Webley army revolver. He marveled at its weight and placed it against his forehead to feel the cool of the metal on his fevered brow. He nudged the business end into the soft palate of his mouth and pulled the trigger.

Meanwhile, Loveday and Milla were in the vestry thanking the new Reverend for his sermon. A light drizzle had begun to fall. Reverend Peterson had more gravitas than the previous incumbent, a firm handshake and much more rhetoric in the way of hail and brimstone.

Rev Pinkerton had slunk back to Devon with his new bride under a bit of a cloud. His wife was a plain girl, slightly dull of mind, who had carried a torch for him since she was fifteen. Barely eighteen, she gave birth to a fully grown baby, six months after her quiet wedding in the village. Apart from the presiding Reverend from another parish, her parents were the only other attendees. Her father, a brutish, coarse type sat next to his weeping wife who had a livid bruise on her right cheek. He had threatened the reverend that he would put his penis through a mincer and feed it to him if he did not marry his daughter. He did not want the humiliation of his girl being sent to Wellswood or Bodmin. The last girl he had seen in that condition was the wild bitch he had been called on to take to Wellswood. He still had the scar to prove it. The reverend found no reason to think he would not carry out this threat, so solemnly said "I do". They left for Devon that afternoon. The wedding set the course of a five-day binge at The Rose for the father of the bride.

Loveday turned in some surprise to see Dr Franklin standing just inside the lychgate. She lifted her hand in acknowledgement. Something in the way he bowed his head somberly alerted her that all was not well. He had removed his hat and was holding it reverently against his chest. Her smile froze on her face as she walked towards him, a cold dread now gripping her stomach at the sight of his grave face. He managed to catch her as she collapsed at the news. The Reverend left his post and helped to place her in Dr Franklin's car.

Milla had not moved. The scene unfolded in front of her as if she were watching a play. One that she would revisit, scene by scene, in the years to come. Her life before, and her life after. The ordinariness of the morning. Sunday service, the same as every Sunday she could ever remember, except when she had the chicken pox. The grey drizzle sweeping past the vestry. Her niggling concern that the rain would ruin her dress. The smell from the lilies on the stone shelf of the nave. Dr Franklin at the lychgate, cap in hand. The collapse of her mother. The mud on the back of her tapestry coat. The open car door and the doctor and the reverend arranging mother onto the red leather back seat. The cold shiver that overcame her as bile rose in her throat, an acid flow from the pit of her stomach deposited over the gravestone of John and Catherine Lytton. A day that marked the end of her old life and left behind a scar that never healed.

Charles Demengel left more than a blood and brain membrane stain on the wall behind his desk that splattered and spread like a Rorschach ink blot test. His abdication of duty to the Celyn estate meant that the finances were in disarray. Loveday had never concerned herself with the running costs of the estate and had assumed the purse would always be full as she indulged her passion for fashionable clothes and a lavish lifestyle. She never even considered the possibility of diminishing funds. It took Theo to sit her down and brutally explain the harsh reality of their situation. The whole house of cards was about to implode. Celyn Lodge would eventually have to be sold. Even once it was stripped of all its assets, the running costs would be unsustainable. There would have to be something of a marriage fire sale for Emmeline and Milla before the full extent of the Demengel nosedive into obscurity would begin.

Most of the staff were let go. The war had seen most of the younger men leave anyway, but it was a devastating blow for many of those who hadn't gone to war. Celyn Lodge had always been a safe bet for employment; its loss was a bitter day, and not just for the family. Loveday insisted that Ted and Cally Newby stayed on in the lodge cottage; deaf to the protestations of Theo. Theo could not understand such an extravagance. Young Joff negotiated himself a position to stay on for bed and board, to maintain the gardens up until the inevitable end. They managed to cling on until just after the war had ended. The proceeds of the paintings, the Persian rugs and the silver had allowed the household to limp on through those lean years. Celyn Lodge was now an empty shell like a carcass stripped bare by vultures.

Lowering her sights and abandoning her hopes of advantageous marriages for her girls, Emmeline had accepted a marriage arrangement from a farmer and landowner from Morwenstow in 1942. Arthur Thatcher had been on the periphery of the elite crowd that Emmeline had partied with before the war.

He was unremarkable and willing to overlook the scandalous suicide of Charles Demengel to bag himself a beautiful wife. He told Loveday he was prepared to fall on his sword and relieve the family of one of the Demengel daughters. Loveday swallowed her fury as well as her pride and acceded to his audacious proposal. He was not, however, able to overlook her appetite for every strong looking farmhand she debased herself with. Slaps rapidly turned into punches, punches into kicks and kicks into one final chokehold that deprived her of breath and led him to a four-year sentence. The judge had been ready to issue the death penalty, then commuted to a life sentence, then to four years when he heard what poor Arthur had endured. Her murder was deemed entirely justifiable. A crime of passion. What kind of man would be able to turn a blind eye to his wife acting like a common prostitute? He was as free as a bird by 1954.

Milla had worked tirelessly alongside Joff in the gardens, growing fruit and vegetables where roses and orchids had once grown. She had swapped finery for dungarees with fortitude and grace. It was harder for Joff to push the memories of Lara out of his mind, with Milla no longer wearing her fancy clothes. In her overalls and her hair coming loose from its elastic ties, she resembled Lara more than she ever had before. It had been easy before to forget they were twins.

His mind strayed back to that February evening in 1937. He tried to push the memory away, but it crowded his mind yet again. Joff had been idling away from the main house, hoping to finish work without been detected by Mr. Hargreaves. He leant against a tree, got out his rolling tobacco and was curling the paper around the strands of tobacco when he saw the girl again. She was riding her horse towards the cottage she shared with that old lady. Her long hair streamed behind her as she drove the horse on. He had seen her before and tried to say hello, but she had not responded.

Impulsively, he stepped in front of the horse. Solomon reared up, unseated Lara, and deposited her on the ground. She raised her eyes to see Joff looking at her. Bloody idiot, she thought, but then recognised the burning look in his eyes she had seen so many times before; the high colour in his cheeks and the bulge pushing against his trousers.

Joff knew with a hideous certainty what he was going to do. He shut out the voice of the Reverend and his mother and knelt between Lara's legs. He undid the rope that held up his trousers. He had expected a struggle, maybe a scream, a scratch or two. What he had not expected was for Lara to yield herself so completely, so sweetly to him, pushing her hips to meet his. And stroking his hair when he slumped on top of her with heaving gasps.

She waited patiently for the slowing of his breath and for him to roll off her. She jumped up easily and wiped up the sticky mess that was now running down her leg with the corner of her skirt.

Without uttering a word or even a backward glance at Joff, she got back on Solomon and rode homeward.

Joff lay there for some time, self-loathing creeping in and chasing away his ecstasy with alarming speed. He retrieved his tobacco and remade his cigarette. The incident was now branded in his mind forever, like an unwelcome visitor. He was appalled at his own depravity. Every time his hands touched Milla's, as he showed her how to plant or twine or dig, he was reminded of the shame of his deed. Like a mutoscope he had seen once at the travelling fair, when he had paid a penny to see what the butler saw; his memories of that moment would come back to haunt him. Unbidden, the memory of a freckled knee. He would pitch his spade harder into the earth to exorcise the unwanted recollection. His nose buried in her salty hair. Dig. A small pink capped breast. Dig. The sharpness of her bony hip colliding with his. Dig. His own ragged breathing. Dig. Her resignation as she waited for him to recuperate. Dig. Her small fingers stroking his head. Dig. Her riding away from him. Forever. Dig.

Lara had disappeared without trace after the night she and Nancy had been found on the beach, Nancy stone dead. He met a wall of silence when he asked. Even Cally Newby would not be drawn on the subject. Cally knew everybody's business and if she didn't know, she would make it up. His life was duller without the hope of another chance encounter, a glimpse of her riding by or picking herbs from the little kitchen garden outside of the cottage. His only comfort was that he would not have to face any consequences for his dark misdeeds.

One late summer's day in 1943, Joff had imagined he was comfortable enough with Milla to ask about Lara's fate. Milla stood and brushed the earth from her knees. She carefully placed the trowel down which moments before she had been using, burrowing into the ground to extricate the late potatoes. She turned on her heel and strode towards Celyn's kitchen entrance. Joff berated himself for misjudging their familiarity and returned to his task, angrily driving his spade into the ground.

The next morning, the familiar sight of Dr Franklin's car drove up to the entrance of Celyn. Loveday and Milla walked towards the car. Milla handed a small suitcase to the doctor who placed it in the back seat. Loveday embraced her daughter tightly. She looked visibly distraught and was unable to stem the flow of tears falling down her face, aged now with sorrow. Joff watched as the car rolled over the gravel, away from Celyn, away from him. Dr Franklin was taking her to

Penzance station to catch the train to Paddington where she would begin her training as a nurse at St. Thomas's Hospital, as part of the war effort. Dr Franklin had been able to pull a few strings to facilitate an immediate start. They were desperate for more hands, so the formalities were cursory. The death of her father weighed heavily on her. She was keen to try and ease the burden of active servicemen by doing everything she could to become a competent and kind nurse. She devoured the written works of Florence Nightingale, her notes on nursing becoming her guiding light in her work. She decided to devote her life to nursing and avoid the common pitfalls of marriage and children. She had seen how precarious it was to be dependent on a husband and children to provide security and contentment.

Theo stayed behind with Loveday whilst Bertie was billeted somewhere in France. Their father's death had sobered them both up. They had both gone to sign up, with Bertie going off for training within 72 hours and Theo returning home with an exemption certificate due to asthma. He had felt mortified and guilty as he saw the eligible population of young men leave Landscove in swathes to battle the enemy. He later felt gratitude that he had a legitimate excuse to stay home as the telegrams streamed in telling mothers their sons were missing or killed in action.

At the end of June 1944, Loveday received a telegram of her own. Bertie was among those who had fallen on June 6th, D-Day. Her dear boy. Her firstborn. She could not reconcile herself to the fact that she would never see his beloved face again. She took to her bed until just before Christmas when she abruptly got up and dressed.

She wandered down to the kitchen and scoured the cupboards for food. She found some cold chicken and biscuits which she devoured hurriedly. She pulled an old coat of Charles' around her, put a pair of boots on, and headed towards the beach. Bowing her head against the cold wind now, she pulled the sleeves of her jumper over her hands to warm them. The breakers were huge, swollen glass mountains today and they roared with a deafening crash up the shore. Her mind began to clear; the fog of the last few months began to dissipate. She had a plan. She lingered a while longer and let the sea spray cascade on her face. With renewed vigour, she made her way back to Celyn and the drawing room. She had barely been in there since Charles had ended his own life so violently. Pushing those thoughts away, she found her writing paper.

Celyn Lodge

Landscove

December 1944

To whom it may concern.

Regarding Lara Demengel

On the envelope, in her sloping hand, she wrote

Wellswood Hospital

Mallock

Cornwall

She then telephoned Dr Franklin and asked him to come and see her.

Dr Franklin had visited Loveday twice a week since she had received news of Bertie. His devotion had little to do with the Hippocratic oath and everything to do with being hopelessly in love with her. He was almost 70 now and knew the Demengel tragedies had bestowed upon him advantages he could not have hoped for had they not occurred. His marriage proposal had sounded more like a rescue package. Loveday had declined, of course. He was 14 years her senior and the thought of having to be intimate with him made her nauseous. This pragmatic decision she had reached during her epiphany on the beach was borne out of a fear of bottoming out completely. To become Mrs. Franklin would mean she wouldn't have to work or starve. It was a compromise of course. She would have to learn to tolerate his advances and hope prevailed he would have an early demise, like his father before him. Swallowing her distaste, she said to an elated Dr Franklin that if the offer still stood, she would become his wife.

In February, in a small ceremony at St. Bede's, the Reverend Peterson pronounced them man and wife. Emmeline had travelled from Morwenstow alone for the occasion. They returned to Celyn and Loveday took her small trunk of belongings to Fore Street to start the next chapter of her life.

Theo and Emmeline sat in the kitchen. Theo put a pan of milk on the range to make cocoa. Emmeline marvelled that Theo knew how to warm a pan of milk up and they both laughed.

"Do you remember Lara would always be hiding out here? With Nancy?"

"I can't remember ever coming down here before the war. I didn't even think about what happened down here, how our eggs and bacon even made their way up to the dining room!" Theo replied.

"Where did Lara go, do you think Theo?"

"I try not to think of her. It just makes me bloody angry. I blame her for father's death. She caused them both so much pain. Little trollop. Do you know there were rumours of her behaving like a complete jezebel in the village before she disappeared? Nancy had no control over her whatsoever. They should have put her away when she was a child."

Emmeline blushed, thinking of her own impropriety.

"Quite," she agreed without conviction.

Emmeline left for Morwenstow the following morning. She took a tour around Celyn for the last time.

"Did you know Celyn is Welsh for holly, Theo?" she said as she got into her car to drive home. She took one more look at the splendid house and sped off for home and the inevitable relentless questioning from Arthur about who she had slept with at the wedding.

Theo packed up the rest of the house before making his final journey through the front gateposts, closing that chapter of his life. There was only one place he could go. Realising he felt unburdened and free, Theo rode his bike the seven miles to Chelston Manor. He felt like he was breaking free of the shackles of tradition and duty. His spirits lifted as he got closer to the love of his life since he was 13. His trunk had been sent on before him, but he had wanted to keep his bicycle. The exercise was good for his asthma, he had decided. Exhausted, he reached the front door of Chelston.

Ernest Blackledge was there to greet him and welcome him with a warm handshake. Theo strained to see if Alex was in the hallway.

"Ah I see Alex is here to show you to your room. Good, good, I will leave you both to it. "

Theo's heart thumped loudly in his chest, partly from the exertion and partly due to being here at last, under the same roof as Alex.

"Let's be having you then," Alex said, and leapt up the stairs like a gazelle, three at a time.

Alex opened the door and pulled Theo in with a theatrical sweep of the arms. Once inside the bedroom, Theo pushed Alex against the door jamb. He ran his hand through Alex's blond hair that hung across his forehead like a curtain.

He looked fully into Alex's face before passionately kissing the open mouth.

"Oh, you beautiful boy," Theo whispered, as they made their way across the floor to the bed.

Chapter 23

Cally and Ted had also had to leave Celyn and return to Ted's mother's house. There was a change in fortunes in that her mother-in-law now needed nursing care. It meant Ted and Cally could spread themselves through the rest of the house and mother was now confined to one room. She had ceased her criticism of Cally, and a new understanding had developed between them. She was also now a Grandmother; a role she relished. Sweet Louise was a little ray of sunshine, her funny gummy smile bringing some much-needed joy into her life. Louise would sit on the chair and look at books and play dolls while Cally rushed around looking after everyone. She cleaned now at Dr Franklin's over at Fore Street three times a week. For the good doctor, and the toff from Celyn who would never be a villager.

Loveday had tried to integrate into village life. She had asked if she could help with arranging the flowers at St. Bede's which led to a lot of ill feeling from Mrs. Wills, who had faithfully bedecked the church for years. Conversation stopped abruptly when she went to the village stores and restarted when the bell signaled her departure.

She stopped trying. One day, she was bored and restless. Cally had gone for the day and Dr Franklin was on his rounds. "I am completely redundant," she thought. Her children were gone. Bertie was cold in the ground, Theo was in Chelston and Emmeline and Milla had their own lives. Even Lara has her own life away from her. She saw her grandchild passing the house from time to time, usually running around as if she was in a pack. She had seen her laughing as one of the Hollis boys ran with her on his back. Piggyback she recalled it being called. She looked like Lara, and Milla of course. Had she not taken the course of action she had, that little girl might be company for herself she thought ruefully. It was too late. She had seen the look of hostility from Tabitha at the May Fayre on the Green. She had stood in front of the child, practically baring her teeth when she walked past with the doctor.

Loveday absently picked up her husband's heavy decanter of whiskey and poured herself a generous slug. She gagged on the first mouthful but persevered. She liked the feeling of warmth and detachment she felt as it coursed through her body. No longer bored, she drank another tumbler full.

Feeling reckless now, she wandered into Dr Franklin's consulting room. It smelled mildly of urine and disinfectant. He had rows and rows of medical journals, Diseases of Modern life, Immunology, Hutchison's Physiology and Hygiene... Tedious beyond belief, she thought.

She looked at the medication cabinet on the wall. It was open. Flinging wide the doors, she surveyed the contents. There were brown bottles of pills and tinctures. One had a sticky residue on the bottle neck. She opened it up; the smell was overwhelming, and she hastily returned it. Loveday was lurching by now, the whiskey rendering her incapable of standing upright. She giggled to herself that she had never thought to do this before. For the first time she understood why Charles lost himself in this way every day since he had returned to Celyn, his essence stolen from him by the trenches of France. She gauged that Dr Franklin would not be home for a few hours. Perhaps she could have a little nap before he came home. She wondered if the good doctor had anything to help her sleep. She was sure she recognised the name Nembutal as one of the medications Dr Franklin had employed as a chemical cosh for Lara back in the day. Picking up her whiskey and the tablets, Loveday swayed to the bedroom.

"Chamber of doom," she laughed to herself bitterly. A little rest and then I will fix him a simple tea. Cally had left some cold meats for her to assemble, having never got to grips with cooking herself.

Loveday threw two of the tablets to the back of her throat and swallowed hard. They were bitter. She was still awake a few moments later and doubted their efficacy. Four more should do it she said cheerfully, hurling the others "down the hatch".

Loveday lay on top of the bed. She did not want to lie down for too long and did not want to remake the bed Cally had so expertly made earlier. She lay down and was aware her breathing was slowing down. Despite closing her eyes, the room still spun. A wave of nausea swept through her. She tried to turn but felt leaden, incapable of movement. Heavy now, a numbness crept up from her toes to her head. And then, like a shutter coming down, an impenetrable darkness fell. Her breathing slowed, and then stopped.

Dr Franklin whistled a little tune. He had been so content since bagging himself a society bride. The war and Charles's death had worked rather favourably for him. It created a level playing field, so to speak. He knew Loveday would never have agreed to marry him without the downfall in her fortunes. He saw in the mirror his sallow complexion and his jowls like soft little pillows of flesh hanging from what had once been a jawline. He knew the hair on his head had somehow been transplanted to his nostrils and ears, and even to his earlobes. When he pulled his lips apart, he saw the yellowing teeth, like ancient piano keys. None of that mattered, with Loveday to accompany him to church and take the occasional turn around the village. He took every opportunity to call her Mrs. Franklin, the name bringing fresh joy to his soul. Every morning as she woke, he would lean across and say "Good morning Mrs. Franklin," as if he couldn't quite believe his good fortune that she was lying beside him. Loveday would stiffen as she tried not to breathe in his putrid breath. The villagers had smirked about the spring in his step and spitefully reveled in the ruination of Mrs. Loveday Demengel. The family pew in St. Bede's was now occupied by whoever arrived first. The Pledge family slid in the pew on that first Sunday after the Franklin wedding. They had stared defiantly ahead when Mr. and Mrs. Franklin had deigned to try and sit there. It was Loveday who motioned for Dr Franklin to accept a back pew, rigid with mortification and defeat and not wanting to draw any more attention than necessary. Most of the families of Landscove had been employed at Celyn at some point.

"Shame she was such a bitch of a mistress then," was the consensus. She had not actively been a dreadful mistress. It was more by omission than commission; she was regarded as a cold fish. The staff were invisible to her. She rarely asked names and had no interest in the lives of the people who worked for her household. She rarely said please or thank you. Her only concern was that they danced attendance to the family and the household ran smoothly. When, by necessity, she did have to liaise with staff, it was always businesslike; no frills or niceties, which ensured the gulf between those who serve and those who were served was maintained.

"Mrs. Franklin," he called, as he hung his coat and hat on the hallstand. He glanced quickly in the small hallstand mirror and smoothed down the few strands of hair that remained. He did not want to greet his wife with hat hair. Cally had been, he noted with a deepening sense of satisfaction with his upturn in circumstances. The hallway smelled of beeswax polish and she had placed some pretty freesias in a jug on the sideboard. Now where was this woman? She had become a bit insular the last few weeks. She had not been a big hit with the ladies in the village, it was true, but he was sure they would warm to her eventually. In the dining room, he noted the lid of his crystal decanter on the floor. How remiss of Cally; I will have to have a word he thought, replacing the glass globe back into its hole. He wandered into the kitchen knowing finding her here was unlikely unless she went in for water. She had not really got to grips with the whole domestic expectations that came with being a doctor's wife without staff. None of that mattered to him. He was more than happy to relinquish a good meal in favour of his treasure, his Loveday.

He climbed the stairs, hoping to find her having an evening bath with a rising hopeful expectation that she might accede to his advances tonight. He entered the bedroom. Laying as if asleep, but obviously stone dead, he keened hopelessly over her, wishing with every fibre of his being she would warm up and come back to him. He tenderly wiped away the trail of vomit that had now dried onto the pillow. Kissing her now, he smelled whiskey. Loveday was not a big drinker, never had been. In fact, since Charles had left the family for the bottle, she seemed to have become averse to the notion of alcohol. So why? Tipped on its side was the small brown bottle. Nembutal. Oh no, no, surely not. Not my Loveday. He could not take it in. He felt numb. Nothing. His mind was a blank. She needed laying out, his professional head told him. But for now, he simply wanted to reimagine his evening. Slipping off his shoes, he lay beside her. If love would wake her, she would rise and berate herself for falling asleep in the afternoon and arrange whatever Cally had prepared earlier for both of them. He knew what was ahead. He would forever be known as the doctor whose wife was so unhappy with him, she killed herself. Staying in Landscove would be untenable. He was ruined. But for one more night, he would lay beside her and pretend all was as it should be.

Theo, Emmeline and Milla stood flint faced as the coroner recorded a verdict of suicide. Dr Franklin had already gone, nobody knew where, but number 4 Fore Street had a notice of sale already in situ.

With Celyn gone, Emmeline, Theo and Milla had to huddle in a corner of The Rose. They sat, stricken, as they each nursed a brandy. Milla had to catch the 5pm train to Paddington. Alex had kindly agreed to take her to Penzance station. He had proved himself a good friend to Theo, thought Emmeline. How animated he was compared to his dreadful bore of a brother she thought. She wondered if her life might have been easier had she accepted his attentions in the halcyon days before Daddy decided to exit stage left. Dull and boring may have been preferable to the hell on earth that she now found herself in with Arthur. Emmeline would be driving herself back to Morwenstow and the inescapable inquisition and predictable fight that would follow.

Ted Newby stood at the bar. He was well oiled as Cally would say. He looked over at the shellshocked Demengel family. Them that's left that is. Oh, how the mighty have fallen he thought. What they did to that poor girl. Deserve everything that's coming he thought. He was fair swaying now and clutching precariously to his beer as they assembled themselves to leave.

"The sins of the Father will be laid upon the children," he said audibly. Valiantly, Alex turned back from the group to confront him. Ted laughed nastily, "Have a go you little poofter."

Theo came and led him away by the arm. "Just leave it Alex. Come on."

Milla wondered what Ted had meant by poofter. She had heard the word in London but had never met one. Not in Cornwall, she decided, and dismissed the idea immediately. The man was drunk after all. But the other thing he said about the sins of the Father? She had felt blighted by father's suicide. And now mother. She felt cursed. Was she so unlovable that both her parents had decided they wanted to leave her? She felt intense anger at both of them. She had seen enough of dying now to see how strenuously people clung to life. The desire to survive is so instinctive. She thought how reluctant most were to leave this life behind. She thought about all the stories she had heard about those struggling to survive on the Titanic. She did not think any would just passively lie down in their cabin and patiently await death. To think that both parents chose to relinquish this gift of life mystified her. She would never know that Loveday was merely bored that afternoon. That she had wanted to duck out for a few hours, not for eternity. If only mother had spoken to her. She knew how devastated she was about leaving Celyn and that she hadn't settled into village life. Mother was defensive when Milla asked her if she was sure she wanted to marry Dr Franklin. Milla had suggested, gently of course, that mother be a little more circumspect, keep her powder dry, and see what else came along. Should she have been more forceful? These questions haunted her as the train left Cornwall and rumbled back to London. If only the past were as easy to leave behind.

Alex held Theo all night as he lamented all his losses, mother being the biggest. The closest to her, he recognised that her apparent lack of passionate emotion had been shaped by societal expectation and her desire to conform, to not rock the boat. She had been molded that way. To please, to appear a certain way, to be a model of how to do life nicely. With pretty things and pretty people. Which is why Lara was such an anathema to her. And why, when everything around her crumbled, she did too. He burrowed his head into Alex's armpit, comforted by the familiar scent of sweat and French cologne. Eventually sleep came.

Tabitha had greeted the news of Loveday's death with relief. She felt like a giant weight she did not know she had been carrying was lifted from her. The money to buy her silence had dwindled over the years and would now stop. She did not care. All she worried about was the Demengel curse not infecting Dolly. She was nearly 11 now with no sign of being tainted by her mother's bad blood. Heaven only knew who the father was. She did not bother herself with those details. She loved her as passionately as she did her own brood and Dolly had thrived. She was sweet natured and content, not giving her parents a moment of bother. Tabitha wrestled with telling Dolly the truth of her birth one day. She did not want to shatter her little bubble, scared it would mar her forever and tarnish their close bond. She did not ever want to stop being the beloved mummy. She did not want her to stop bringing home a bunch of wildflowers or painting a picture, just for her. Or for her to stop proudly showing off her achievements like when she first jumped off seal rock into the sea down in the cove. She knew that one day a birth certificate might be required to get married. But not yet. Not today as she read the verdict of the inquest in the Herald.

Chapter 24

October 1950

Emmeline had woken late. She had a migraine threatening, like dark clouds gathering on the horizon. She yearned for the old days of Celyn where she could have summoned up a glass of cool water with a tinkle of a bell. Already, winter was looming. The farmhouse was cold and cheerless upstairs. Pulling her housecoat on, she shivered. The house was quiet, thankfully; Arthur rose early as he did every day to see to the farm. He was also keen on a morning walk which gave Emmeline some much needed time to herself. He was a monster. The time lapse between physical attacks had got shorter and shorter. In the early years, there would be a hiatus between assaults. A slap would be followed by a contrite Arthur, tearful, as he begged her forgiveness. There would be flowers, maybe a little trinket to cement his promise that he would never, ever lay a finger on her again. Emmeline could breathe in the wake of an attack, knowing that whilst her bruises were healing, Arthur would be in repentance mode and she would be left alone. Until the next time. She had learned to recognise the signs. The darkening of his face and the blackness of his eyes. She hated his freckled hands; the same hands that wanted to make love to her as the ones that blacked her eyes. Emmeline realised it did not matter what she did, he would not stop. Even if she became the perfect wife. It slowly dawned on her it was not because she was lazy or a bitch, or a whore, or a worthless nobody. It was because Arthur liked it.

When she realised this, she thought she may as well be hung for a sheep as for a lamb. She did not attempt to curb her appetite for mindless dalliances. She enjoyed the feeling of power it gave her; to make men weak for her. The uglier they were, the more she was worshipped. With no other purpose or passion to amuse her, she would frequently seek out her next opportunity. Her contempt for others was beginning to imprint itself on her face, eroding her looks. She had begun to look sour and angular. Her overriding concern in life was the loss of her charms. She ate barely anything to maintain an unnatural thinness. And despite living on a farm with little in the way of a social life, she was always made up as if she were still in the throng of a social whirl.

"Oh shit," she said aloud, as she reached across the bed and vomited into the jug and bowl on the dresser next to her bed. She lay back on her pillows with the awful certainty dawning on her that she was pregnant. This was the third time this week she had started her day with a spew, and she hadn't bled for 6 weeks, she calculated. There was nothing she could do, nowhere she could go. A divorce was out of the question. There was no longer a home to go to and both of her parents were dead. She was a social pariah, nobody wanting to associate themselves with that breed of bad fortune. Arthur's family loathed her. They found her brittle and she had no concept of what it was to be a farmer's wife.

She was wholly isolated. Earlier that week, her hope had soared when she overheard the stable hand telling Jane Cross there had been an accident on the farm; hoping against hope it was Arthur that was maybe mangled in the plough or had been trampled by a herd of cows. Her disappointment knew no bounds when Arthur came in for lunch and told her one of the farmhands had his arm severed in the thresher. So, she was trapped.

She got up and brushed her teeth to try and get rid of the taste of sick. She breathed into her cupped hand. Overtones of spearmint and puke. She needed water. She made her way to the kitchen. She jumped back in alarm to see Arthur seemingly looking for something in the drawers.

"Finally, up are you? If only I hadn't married such a lazy slut. Lolling about in bed whilst I work to keep a roof over your bitch head".

Ignoring him, Emmeline maneuvered around him and went to fill a glass from the tap.

"Did you hear me? I could have had anyone. Anyone. I rescued you from your degenerate family. And look at you. Ungrateful little bitch."

She turned and looked at him. She took a swig of water.

"Don't sneer at me. You just love winding me up, don't you? Think I would do this to anyone else? A decent girl who could keep her legs shut?"

He came closer. Emmeline braced herself for his blow. She was ready. The anticipation was worse somehow. She decided to speed it along. She just wanted an aspirin and to go back to bed.

"I'm pregnant," she stated matter-of-factly.

Arthur hesitated. He had a nanosecond of delight. A son to take over the farm and pass on the Thatcher name. He would have to be more careful how he hit her for the next nine months. His eyes moved down to her tummy. Emmeline's eyes followed his and she gave a little laugh.

"Oh dear! Poor dear boy. It's not yours. Anyone's guess really, Arthur. Could be Tom, Dick or Harry's," laughing at her little joke for the last time, before Arthur left her bloodied and beaten on the flag tiles of the kitchen where he had finished her off, her eyes bulging like a bullfrog.

PART 3

Chapter 25

"This is really upsetting Mum. I am sorry but I am going to have to ask you to stop. It's okay, Mum." soothed Louise, straightening out her blanket and wiping her face with a tissue. "There's nothing more we can tell you. I'm sorry."

Dr Winstanley stood up. "Of course. We are sorry to have upset her so much." She smoothed down her white trousers, so pristine yesterday but now sporting a splash of ketchup from breakfast.

As they were leaving, Cally straightened herself up in her chair. Like a clearing in a fog, she said, "Dolly isn't dead."

The three women looked at her. "Oh, she is always saying that too. Gawd only knows what she means," she said, as she showed them out.

It was raining when they got back to the car. No open top today. The car was full of condensation Dr Winstanley had to clear before they could return to Wellswood. It was definitely a fair-weather car, Shelley thought as she felt a bit shivery after the warmth of yesterday. They were not dressed for rain. They both nursed some disappointment that they hadn't made more progress about Lara. The letter from Dr Franklin had said the baby died 40 minutes neonatally, most likely to do with a congenital abnormality. They had hoped maybe for a sibling, one that could talk. Emmeline and Bertie were side by side in the churchyard in St. Bede's, Mrs. Loveday Franklin and Charles Demengel separated by a few feet of common ground. Louise had been able to tell them that much. Louise had no idea what had become of either Milla or Theo.

By the time the roadster swung into Wellswood it was dark. Dr Winstanley did not switch the engine off at she let Shelley off outside Bawtree house.

"Thanks Shelley. We did our best. I will see you next week," and off she went, towards home and her family. Shelley felt desperately homesick. I will try and ring Ma tonight.

She went down the long corridor to her room. She turned the key in the door. Someone had pushed a note under her door.

Don't forget payday disco you big giant lezzer. That's if you have finished brown nosing the Doc. Big love, Jules xxx

She smiled as she looked for something suitable to wear.

Chapter 26

Shelley knew the routine well now. As she arrived on the ward, she checked in to report for duty. Sister Berry barely nodded an acknowledgement as she showed her face in the office. Shelley had blotted her copy book and her unfavourable ward report had already been written, despite having another six weeks to go.

The heavy ward curtains had already been opened by the night staff and the tables laid for breakfast. Divesting herself of her cardigan she went to run the three baths. She walked into the dormitory. The smell was always the worst in the morning. Unwashed bodies, fetid morning breath and the lingering cloud of flatulence as quilts were thrown back.

The "ambulants" now threaded their way to the bathroom. Some took their own nightdresses off and stepped into the waiting bath, and some stood passively with arms up, waiting for help. These quickies were done first, before being sent along the line to be dried. The others, "the babies", needed more help and would be left until last.

Shelley had bathed eight patients and passed them down the human conveyer belt. She was amazed to have woken up at all. She had only planned to have the one drink to show her face. But they had found a fellow countryman for her, a lad called Sean, and she ended up having a great night. He said he was supposed to have started last week but had got so pissed on the ferry he had stayed over in Holyhead for a few days, enjoying the hostelries of North Wales. He was hoping to do his training but for now had got himself a job as a nursing assistant. It was lovely to see and hear someone from near home. It was the messiest night she had had out since she left home, Lara far from her mind.

She was waiting for the next patient when she had a wave of nausea. Her mouth filled with water. She rested her head on the cool porcelain of the bath. Whatever possessed her to get so drunk before an early? The wave passed. She hoped a bit of breakfast might quell the nausea.

Last bath completed she went to help with the breakfast.

"Morning Janet. I hope you are feeling better," Shelley enunciated all her words and spoke very clearly to help Janet lip read.

"Bloody hell Shelley. Don't know what you have been told but I am not that deaf!"

"Janet I am so sorry. I didn't mean to be patronising."

Janet laughed. "Don't worry about it. I am hard of hearing, but I am pretty good with lip reading. But just talk normally for goodness's sake. And don't turn your back on me!"

Quietly now, Janet said, "Thank you for being kind last week. I just couldn't take any more. The pair of them are unbelievable. That brute sat and watched Slater terrorising poor Eva for a full hour until Grace spoilt their fun by having a fit. Eva was hysterical, poor girl. When I gave Slater a dirty look, she told me to get over myself, it was only a bit of fun. We would all go mad if we didn't have a bit of a laugh now and again, she said."

"Janet. Would you be willing to write that up? Like a bit of a report?"

After a moment, she said she couldn't. Her and her husband worked in the hospital. Their name would be mud and they needed the work.

"If you change your mind?"

"I will come to you first".

A new alliance was forged.

Breakfast was over and Mr. Scott was just leaving the villa. Sister Berry was simpering around him and collected his coat from the office. She smiled up at him and he looked at her with naked admiration. Her smile was fixed as she closed the door behind him, but it slipped when she saw Shelley.

"A word, Merrigan," she said.

Shelley followed her into the office. Sister Berry sat in her chair behind the desk and leaned back, regarding her coolly.

"I hear you had a day out with Dr Winstanley? I didn't realise you two were such good friends."

Shelley did not know how to answer so she stayed silent.

"Don't forget what I told you before, Merrigan. You can have it hard. Or a smooth ride. Your shout. But I warn you, cross me at your peril. Now. Get me a coffee. I am doing the off duty now, so I need some caffeine."

She had been dismissed.

After she had given Sister Berry her coffee, she was going to re-stock the linen trolley to make beds. The doors to the dormitory and the bathrooms were adjacent. Shelley could hear a tap running. Ah, I am never drinking on a school night again she thought. I am not on my A game; I must have left the tap on.

She walked down the corridor towards the bathroom. She could hear a whimpering sound. She stopped briefly and tried to strain her ears towards the sound. What on earth was it? She thought perhaps a cat had got in through an open window. There were plenty of feral cats around the villas at night; she had jumped in alarm before, seeing their glassy eyes beneath the glare of her little torchlight. Cautiously she walked towards the sound. She was not crazy about cats really and was scared it might jump up and scratch her. The whimpering was louder as she got closer to the source of the noise. And then the most guttural, primal noise she had ever heard pierced the air. "NOOOOOO," Lara screamed as she pushed Nurse Slater into the wall. There was a sickening crack as she hit her head on the sink on the way to the floor. Lara had pushed her as easily as if she were a skittle. Nurse Slater's legs splayed beneath her and blood began to fan out underneath her head. The whimpering had abated. Pammy was curled up on the cold bathroom tiled floor like a hedgehog. Shelley and Lara looked at each other for the longest time.

"Lara, go. Go quickly to your room."

Lara did not move.

"Lara. Please." Shelley implored her. "Trust me. Go to your room. I promise you I will sort this out."

Lara crept away quietly, with no hint of panic, or hurry. Or regret, Shelley noted.

Shelley got to work quickly. She gently picked Pammy up from the floor, warming her with towels. She was freezing. Nurse Slater had been dousing her with cold water from the tap, using the Tupperware jug used for hair washing. The pool of blood was spreading. Shelley had never seen a dead person before. She could not be one hundred percent sure she was not just unconscious. But she was sure nobody could lose that amount of blood and survive. She found a dress and a cardigan that Nurse Slater must have discarded before she started her game with Pammy. Sitting Pammy down in one of the wheelchairs that were lined up in the ante bathroom now. She stroked her cheek to let her know she was safe.

That 'oul bitch will never touch you again Pammy."

The floor was wet. Shelley added a little shampoo to the mix to make it look more hazardous. She did not need to move Nurse Slater. A dreadful accident at work that would find its way into the health and safety at work manual. The importance of prompt attendance to spills. Trips and slips hazards. Shelley smiled inside every time she saw that directive over the years.

Satisfied she had secured the scene; she started to scream and call for help. She had to imagine it was her ma bleeding on the floor to get the pitch just right. She could step back once the cavalry arrived. Nobody was looking at her now, they were focused on the sight of Nurse Slater with her mouth in the shape of a shocked "oh". Sister Berry kicked into action, feeling her pulse on the side of her neck; an impotent act as even to Shelley's limited experiences of death, this woman was probably already in hell.

Some of the patients drawn by the noise had gathered around.

"Get them out of here and get help, Merrigan. Now. Move." Shelley shepherded them all into the dayroom.

She turned the radio up louder. She went to the office and dialled 9999 for the internal emergency team.

Nurse Slater left Cypress for her final time on a trolley in a nylon body bag. Shelley thought it looked like the same kind of bag her Ma's dry cleaning came back in with her dress for her annual dinner dance at the working man's social club. Shelley was surprised not to see Sketchley's emblazoned across it.

"Clear the way, I thought I told you to get this lot cleared off!" Sister Berry barked, as she tried to give her friend a shred of dignity.

Shelley did as she was told. It was only Lara who remained to see the double doors open to the sunshine beyond. As she was lowered down the ramp, Shelley caught Lara's eye. She was beaming. She made no effort to hide her delight from Shelley. Not until the trolley was on its trajectory to the hospital morgue did she return to her room. Mr. Scott and Sister Berry were in the office now, heads bowed close. With a light heart, Shelley and Pippa Burrows, nursing assistant, muddled on as best they could. Pippa was red eyed and kept bursting into tears. Shockwaves rippled through the ward. Shelley had to keep reminding herself not to be jubilant. Soon a new staff nurse was drafted in from Ivy ward and stoically led the rest of the shift. Sister Berry's husband had come to pick her up. The bathroom had been cleared. Two stains removed in one day thought Shelley.

Just before the end of the shift, Staff Nurse Crisp summoned Shelley into the office.

"Student Nurse Merrigan. I know you have already been asked to write your statement. You found her first, right? I just want to make sure you are feeling okay before you go home. Do you live in?"

Shelley nodded.

"Is there anyone who can support you? You are a long way from home. Irish, right?"

Shelley hoped Julie was around to join her in a massive drink as soon as the social club opened at 5pm. Her hangover wasn't forgotten, but a bit of hair of the dog would not go amiss. She reassured the nurse she would be fine. As she pulled her cardigan off the coat hook, she blurted out, "I couldn't stand the fecking old bitch if the truth be told."

The staff nurse smiled wryly, "Maybe best to keep that to yourself! But yeah. Could not have happened to a nicer person. She was a perverse demonic pig of a woman."

"Oh, don't look so shocked Merrigan! I was a student once too. I tried to report her, but nothing happened except I got moved to another ward. And got a shit report. Keep your side of the street clean. Always. These women are someone's child, sister, cousin, aunt. Don't ever forget that."

"Thanks. Thanks so much." As she walked back to Bawtree House, she thought there might be some good in this place after all. A glimmer of hope started to germinate within her. She could make a difference after all.

PART 4

Chapter 27

August 1957

Dolly walked down towards the cove. It was early; she had not wanted to wake Daniel so had crept out of the house. She had slung a towel over her shoulder and crossed the scrubby grass towards the sand. Dolly had wanted their little beach side cottage from when she had first seen it as a child. It had not been occupied for years when they bought it at a knockdown price.

"It's cheap because nobody in their right mind would want to live there," Tabitha had said. It was true. Green, wet algae crept up the walls. It was exposed to the elements and had been neglected. But Dolly needed the ocean like others need oxygen. She swam every opportunity she got. She had long exceeded the skills of her brothers and sisters. Her family called her the mermaid. But Dolly didn't want to live anywhere else, and Daniel would do anything to make her happy. They had already made it damp proof, and Dolly had made a sweet dwelling for them both. She liked to collect seashells and driftwood and surprised herself with her skills at bringing the cottage back to life. Tabitha had been sewing and embroidering for her girls for years, so the fishing nets and lobster pots were cleared out and replaced with cushions and curtains.

Tabitha had worried when Dolly started to moon about Daniel Lane when she was only 15. He was twenty and she worried why he would be interested in a girl so young. It had taken time for her to warm to him. With his dark looks and almost black eyes, she was anxious he would break her heart. Five years later, she realised she had no cause for concern. Daniel took over the mantel from her husband; he worshipped Dolly.

Dolly had ballooned in the last two weeks of her pregnancy and her legs felt like she was wearing tight wellingtons. She wondered whether her ankles were still there under all the swelling. Her abdomen was so distorted, so alien to her. She was shocked every time she caught her reflection. Could that really be her?

Just another two weeks to go. She felt ready for it now, although she was nervous about the birth and whether she would be a good mum. Tabitha assured her she would be fine, and Nanna would be just a little holler away if she needed anything. The doctor had said she was carrying a lot of water. She had felt more tired than she could ever had thought possible. But she was nearly there.

She slipped her sundress over her head. The beach was deserted at this time of the morning. There was a gentle wave today. She walked in and propelled herself forward when she was deep enough to swim. Oh, the sweet relief of the cold water; a hot day was promised, and she knew this would keep her cool for a few hours. She swam slowly, the peaks and troughs of the waves lifting her gently. She was weightless; she felt like a seal.

Cumbersome on land but graceful in the water. She lay back in the water and looked up at the cloudless sky. She felt the rumble of the sea in her ears, felt it reverberate through her body. The water had done its work; she felt renewed.

Dolly came out of the water and wiped her face with the towel. She pulled the dress back over her head, knowing she would be dry in moments. Gingerly she sat down, wondering if that were a good idea, if she would be able to get back up. She had not expected to get that big.

Mesmerised by the waves, she thought about Tabitha and the sacrifices she had made for her. For all of them. If I am just a fraction of the Mum she has been, this baby will be so lucky.

Dolly thought about that day two years ago when Daniel had gone to ask her Dad for her hand in marriage. Dad's face had clouded. She knew Daniel was five years older, but he was hard working and reliable. "I need to speak to your mother."

Half an hour later, Ross and Daniel had gone to the Rose, and Tabitha led Dolly by the hand into the kitchen. Tabitha looked pale and tremulous. Dolly had no idea why her mother looked so distraught. She thought they had come round to the idea of her and Daniel being together.

Before her on the table was a biscuit tin she had not seen before. Tabitha kept her hands on it, her knuckles turning white.

"This is the moment I have dreaded for eighteen years. Dolly, what I am about to tell you doesn't change anything. Me and your Dad love you, always have, always will. No matter what. I hope you know that."

Getting scared now, Dolly said of course she knew.

"Have you ever wondered that you don't look like your brothers and sisters?"

"Oh that? Because I'm adopted?"

"You knew?"

"Well, I wasn't sure. I did wonder but Todd blurted it out when he was lagging one night. Years ago, now Mum. I figured you would tell me in your own good time. I have always felt so loved I wasn't really interested in who gave birth to me. You are my real Mum and Dad. I love you both so much. Isn't that all that matters?"

Tabitha pulled her into a tight embrace. What had she done so right to be blessed with this child? She lifted the lid of the biscuit tin, a bit like a Pandora's box she thought. A small brown envelope lay at the bottom. She unfolded the pleated piece of paper and pushed it across the table for Dolly to read. It was her birth certificate. Mother: Lara Demengel Father: Unknown. Dr Franklin had given her the certificate along with the money for her keep and strict instructions to keep it hidden and secret.

Tabitha did not know for sure where Lara had been taken or indeed whether she was still alive. She feared asking questions might jinx everything and Dolly would be taken from them. But Tabitha wanted Dolly to understand that despite everything, her mother would have kept her if she could. That she had fought to stop Dolly been taken away. That she had seen the passionate love she had had for her new baby. As gently as she could, she told Dolly that Lara had been considered odd. She had been shunned by her family and raised by the cook in a cottage in the grounds of Celyn Lodge.

And that she had been called upon to deliver her into the world and had loved her from that first moment.

"Does that mean I can marry Daniel now?"

Dolly had only started thinking about her birth mother as her pregnancy progressed. She felt sorry for her and hoped wherever she was, she was happy. She stroked her abdomen and stood up clumsily to stroll the short way home. Daniel was up. She kissed him and cupped his handsome face in hers.

"Mm. Salty. Nice swim?"

"Yes. Now to get this place sorted. I am feeling full of beans and bus tickets as Dad would say."

By the next morning, her twin boys lay side by side in the little crib for one. The water she was carrying was another baby. They were a good size for twins, just over 4lb each. Dolly could not take her eyes off them. They were perfect. Tabitha had been there as well as Dr Wilson. Everything was straightforward despite the unexpected second baby.

"Jack and Dylan."

"They are carbon copies of you Dolly," Tabitha said. A shock of black hair, navy eyes and Jack had a tiny birthmark under his right eye.

"It looks like a star," Dolly said. It was the only distinguishing feature that helped to tell one from the other. Daniel looked at his little family and made a silent vow to protect them until his dying breath.

Chapter 28

Sister Berry was still off sick, and Staff Nurse Crisp was still providing temporary cover on Cypress. The charged atmosphere had gone, and instinctively the patients seemed to have sensed a sea change. They still cowered when staff approached, but that was to be expected, Nurse Crisp had said.

"We just need a consistency of approach. Calm, kind and confident." Nurse Crisp poached one of the nursing assistants from Ivy. "I have told that moron Scott I don't want any of the old Cypress staff on here".

Shelley had to search for the accident book when Janet sliced her finger on a sharp knife in the washing up bowl. Before, it was on the desk by the diary, it was in use so frequently. It was full of entries by Sister Berry and Nurse Slater. Shelley felt sick as she looked at the entry for the ladle attack on Grace that they had passed off as a seizure. She wished she had possessed Lara's courage and done something to stop them herself.

There was no change in Lara's behaviour. She wandered around the ward like a spirit, apparently oblivious to her surroundings. Dr Winstanley was due at 11 today to see her. Shelley had omitted to tell her about what she had seen and heard on that morning. She had a sleepless night wondering what she should do. She was afraid the doctor may be duty bound to investigate thoroughly and she worried that Lara might be recommitted to Beech. No, she would tuck this secret tightly into her heart forever. It would remain between her, Lara and God.

The villa doors had been wedged open to create a through draft. Nurse Crisp and Shelley had arranged some chairs on the veranda so patients could get some air.

"Don't let anyone on Largactil sit in the sun, Shelley," Nurse Crisp reminded her. "A bit of fresh air is fine, but we don't want any sunburn."

Shelley lifted her hand in greeting to Dr Winstanley as she made her way towards them. She trod on her cigarette butt and blew the smoke upwards.

"Good morning Doctor. Nurse Merrigan tells me you are here to see Lara? Fascinating. More to her than meets the eye I reckon. Let me know if I can help at all."

Shelley and Dr Winstanley went into the quiet room.

"Shelley, I have heard that Sister Berry is due back. We are going to have to act now. Expose her. I don't want her to ever work near a vulnerable patient again. Have you got the journal"?

Emboldened now by Lara's fearless act, she said yes. She was ready, even if that meant her hanging up her nurses' uniform for ever and returning to Ireland.

"Nurse Crisp? Can we trust her?"

"I think we can," Shelley said.

"Ok. First let us see Lara. Would you mind getting her?"

Shelley knocked on the door. Lara jumped up from her bed and opened the door. Tiny Tears was on the bed. She made no move to hide her from Shelley. She opened the bottom drawer of the 3-drawer chest where she had fashioned a little nest for her doll from tea towels from the kitchen. She lay the doll down gently and closed the drawer.

"Lara," Shelley said, her voice barely a whisper. Lara looked at her keenly and Shelley knew that she saw her.

"I will never tell. Ever. Not even Dr Winstanley. It is between us. I give you my word."

Lara lifted her hand. For one dreadful moment Shelley thought she would strike her. With the back of her fingers, she brushed Shelley's cheek, before making her way to see the doctor.

Chapter 29

Dr Winstanley was startled when the phone rang on her desk. It was Helen from the admin office. She had been on annual leave for two weeks. "I am so sorry Doctor. When you collected those notes the other week? You dropped an envelope. I asked someone to bring it over for you, but it's still here in my "in tray". Honestly, if you want a job doing and all that! Shall I pop it across later?"

"Oh, I'll come and get it now," she said, curiosity propelling her out of the door.

Abruptly cutting across Helen who wanted to resurrect the "How awful about Nurse Slater" narrative, she thanked her and scooted back towards Cherry. The letter had clearly been opened and returned to its envelope at some point.

The letter was on good quality headed paper. The address. Celyn Lodge. On the envelope was written Wellswood Hospital.

December 1944
Wellswood Hospital, Mallock
Re: Lara Demengel.
To whom it may concern.

I am writing regarding my daughter, Lara Demengel. I am entrusting this information to you for you to decide what is in her best interests. I have held a secret for seven years and believe my life has been cursed as a result. My husband died suddenly as war broke out and my son was killed in action at the D-Day landings. This has made me reflect on my own mortality and I do not want to die with this on my conscience.

Maybe if I explain myself, my rationale will be easier to understand. Lara and her twin sister are my youngest children. Lara was always difficult, even as a baby. She was an anomaly within the family; disobedient and unlovable. I regret to say I could not manage her, and she subsequently lived with staff within the grounds of Celyn, although I did maintain contact with her, obviously.

Nobody had any idea she was with child until the day she had the baby. You can imagine my shock and horror at these events. I hid this from my husband as the truth would have destroyed him. He returned from the war a changed man and I felt I needed to shield him from anything that may upset him.

Dr Franklin and I decided it was in Lara's best interests to say the baby had died shortly after birth. I understand Dr Franklin told Lara this on the way to hospital and she then became extremely violent.

Lara could never have taken care of the baby, that was obvious. There was never any question of her being taken care of by the family; it would have destroyed our reputation and the opportunities for my other children.

However, everything is lost. My husband and my beloved son. My whole world is shattered. Soon, I will have to leave Celyn Lodge behind. Anything of worth has been sold. The only thing left is my morality, hence this letter. I will leave it up to your good judgement whether to tell Lara the truth of her baby.

The woman who attended the birth agreed to take the child into her care. Her name is Tabitha Hollis. I understand from Dr Franklin the child is happy and healthy with no sign of the malady that inflicted her mother. They remained in the village of Landscove. I understand they called the child Dolly.

I hope now my family will be able to find peace.

Yours faithfully,
Loveday Demengel.

Dr Winstanley leaned back in her chair and let out the longest sigh. She correctly assumed this letter had been tucked away all these years and Lara never knew her child was alive. How dare they? How dare they keep this from her. Bastards. Pair of bastards. Hope their lives turned to shit, she thought

"Hi Nurse Crisp. Can you spare Shelley for half an hour? Send her over to my office, could you?"

Within 15 minutes, Shelley was sitting in front of Dr Winstanley who was apoplectic with rage. They had both read Dr Franklin's letter that said the baby had died neonatally within a few hours.

"Read and weep," she said, handing over the letter.

"There's a good chance this baby is alive and well and living in Landscove. Now it makes sense. Cally knew! Dolly isn't dead! She was lucid after all. We have got to go back Shelley. We must find Dolly."

Chapter 30

This time they were prepared for a two day stay with an overnight at The Rose. Armed with Loveday's letter they checked in. There was no sign of the heartthrob on this occasion but now there was no time for frivolity; they meant business and had so much to go on. They put their overnight bags in the same twin room they had stayed in before. Dr Winstanley had rung the tea shop and spoken to Louise Gidley a few days before. Reluctantly, she agreed to meet them back at the house. All the doctor had told her was her mum was not totally delusional and she needed to ask more questions.

"I will be as gentle as I can," she promised Louise.

Despite the heat of the day, a fire was burning in the hearth again. There was now a hospital bed wedged into the corner of the room. Louise said her mum had had another mini stroke and had deteriorated even further. Cally lay in bed staring up at the ceiling. There was a snail trail of saliva running from the slack side of her mouth. Her eyes looked more vacant than before. One arm lay flaccid through the bars of the bed, the other hand worrying the sheet. A catheter bag was filling with dark brown urine. Dr Winstanley saw she was on the threshold of death; estimating no more than ten days left. She lightly lay her hand on hers; it felt like the bones of a tiny fragile bird.

"Cally, it's Dr Winstanley again. Vix. You remember I was here some weeks ago? "

Dr Winstanley pressed on.

"She is only making noises now," Louise said.

"Cally. I have a letter here from Loveday Demengel. You worked for her right? At Celyn Lodge? Louise told us last time you lived and worked there for years?"

Cally's good hand worked the sheet, more agitated now.

"She said Lara had a baby. You knew, didn't you?"

"Now come on Doctor. You promised me you wouldn't upset her".

"Ok. Cally. Last time you were here, you said Dolly wasn't dead? Is she still alive? Here in Landscove?"

Cally made a noise as if she were trying to speak.

"Dolly?" asked Louise. "There is a Dolly in Landscove. She has lived here all her life. Married to Daniel Lane?"

Dr Winstanley swiveled to Louise now. "Before she was married. What was her name before she married Daniel?"

"Dolly Hollis. She was bought up just around the corner. Her Mum only died last year. Loads of Hollis's around the village. None of them went far. All devoted to Tabitha they were. "

"Where can I find Dolly?"

"'Spect you will find her by the cove. Lovely place they have got right down on the beach. You will have seen the painting of it hung up in the tea shop. All the artists want to come and paint it. Nobody else wanted it back in the day! Damp fisherman's cottage. You wanna see it now!"

"But Dolly? What can you tell me about her?"

"She was the best-looking girl in the village. Lovely with it, mind. Her and Tabitha were proper close. Nursed her up until her dying day she did. They all did. Who is this Lara? "

"I can't tell you I am afraid. But your mum. She hasn't been talking nonsense. She has really helped us. I cannot thank you enough Louise. For letting us talk to her."

Turning back to Cally now, she spoke gently.

"Cally thank you. You can rest easy now. Everything is going to be fine."

To ease the old woman's passing, she whispered in her ear that Lara and Dolly would be reunited. She would make sure Lara was told about Dolly. She reassured her that she would right the wrongs of the past.

As they were leaving, Louise said they might have come across Dolly's boys. Twins. Jack and Dylan.

"The local heartthrobs! Good boys they are. They work opposite shifts in The Rose."

Chapter 31

Following Louise's instructions, they took the footpath towards the beach. To the right the track veered down towards the house. Nestled by the dunes, there it was. Whitewashed with pale blue shutters at the windows and fronted by a large, bleached wood deck. The chairs and table were made of driftwood. One chair had a pale cashmere blanket strewn casually over one arm and an open book, leaf upwards that made Shelley want to walk into this life. *The L-Shaped Room* by Lynne Reid Banks, Shelley noted, making a mental note to add it to her "must read" list. The table had a jug of dark liquid, not unlike Cally's catheter bag, but with a lemon floating on top of it.

There did not seem to be a bell or a door knocker. It felt intrusive somehow to go onto the deck

"Hello, can I help you?" A smiling woman walked towards the house from the beach, blotting the hair of her ponytail with a stripey towel. She was tanned and bare foot. Her navy eyes were accentuated by her bronzed face and freckles. Effortlessly beautiful, Shelley thought with a tinge of envy. She was one of those women who made her feel like a hulking beast of burden, clumsy and awkward.

"Good morning. Beautiful morning for a swim."

"Absolutely. Wakes me up and clears the cobwebs!"

"You must wonder what we are doing here. Are you Dolly Lane? Previously Hollis?"

Frowning now, Dolly confirmed she was.

Using what Shelley now recognised as her Doctor voice, she went on. She introduced herself and Shelley. She said that what she had come to tell her might be deeply shocking so she might want to sit down. She said they both worked at Wellswood Hospital in Mallock. A hospital for people with a mental handicap, tactfully omitting its real title of hospital for the mentally subnormal. Dolly interrupted her.

"Let me get us all a drink. I can make coffee, or I have a fresh iced tea in the fridge?"

They sat on the deck with iced tea.

Dr Winstanley adopted her professional pose and was about to relaunch into her revelation.

"Is this about Lara? Lara Demengel?" enquired Dolly. "Has she passed away?"

After a few moments of shock, the doctor recovered herself and reassured her quickly that she was very much alive. Dolly told the women everything Tabitha had told her. She told them that according to Tabitha, Lara had held her and nurtured her lovingly for the all too brief time they had together. Tabitha had not known where she was taken. She had not been able to tell her much because she had not met her until the early hours of that morning when she had been awoken from her sleep to go to the cottage in Celyn Lodge. Dolly said fate had been kind to her. She had been raised in a loving family and Tabitha had been a wonderful mother. She had not made any further enquiries into her birth mother out of respect for Tabitha. Obviously, she had thought of her over the years; did she look like her? Did she think of her on her birthday? And when my sons were born it made me think of how awful it must have been to have me ripped from her arms. What would she think if she knew she was a grandmother?

Dolly said she had resigned herself to never knowing. Her family was right here, Daniel and the boys. And of course, her Hollis family with whom she remained close. She had an extraordinary lack of curiosity about the past, the Demengel family and Celyn Lodge. She figured that if they did not want to know about her, they probably were not worthy of her time.

Dr Winstanley asked if she would like to know about Lara. She was careful not to use the term "Mother" as Dolly was clearly fiercely loyal to the memory of Tabitha. Dolly nodded her agreement.

Doctor Winstanley confirmed that she resembled her physically very closely. She told her she was in good physical health.

"Dolly, she doesn't talk, but I believe this is what we call selective mutism."

Shelley reddened. She had not told the doctor she had heard her yelling "no" when she hurled Nurse Slater across the bathroom.

"My best guess is she has a reasonable grasp of language. She appears to understand but there is clearly some level of cognitive impairment that I haven't been able to assess because of her mutism. It is hard to separate out what the effects upon her are, living in an institution for so long. It is what we call institutional neurosis. Basically, she has been treated as less than human. So, some of her behaviours are what you might expect from someone who has been kept away from the outside world for nearly four decades."

Dr Winstanley left out her long incarceration in Beech ward, and her attack on Nurse Treloar. She did not want to alarm or distress her at this juncture. Although, she noted, Dolly was taking all this information in without becoming visibly upset.

"Can I see her?"

The doctor had not anticipated it would be this easy.

"Dolly, Lara was told you had died shortly after birth. I will have to deal with this very carefully and give some thought as to how I handle it. I do not want to destabilise her. But she has a right to know. And I will tell her, of course. Shelley here has built up something of a rapport with Lara. Although she only has a short while before she moves on to her next placement, she will be allowed back to complete her case study and can therefore maintain contact for a bit longer. With both of us as consistent figures, I am confident you can visit soon. I just want to manage your expectations. She may not engage with you at all. She is something of an isolate. She doesn't interact with her fellow patients; most of whom she has shared a space with for many years."

"I will wait to hear from you doctor. And thank you. For finding me and coming all this way to tell me."

She held out her hand to the doctor who irrationally found herself feeling choked up. Looking into this lovely face, so like her mother's. How things could have been so different for them both. But so grateful that Tabitha had been the one called that day. Knowing what little she knew of the Demengels, she had dodged a toxic bullet.

Chapter 32

The dayroom was stifling despite the open windows and wedged open doors. Staff Nurse Crisp hummed along to the radio whilst giving out the medication. The atmosphere was light. Pammy smiled and rocked rhythmically to the music. Olivia came and threw her arms around Nurse Crisp's waist and put her head into her chest.

"Come on now Olivia, that's enough!" Olivia shook her head and tightened her grip. Nurse Crisp laughed and returned the embrace.

"Just a few seconds more missus. These tablets won't give themselves out."

Today was the day. Shelley and Dr Winstanley were going to tell Lara about Dolly. They had discussed it all on the journey back from Landscove. Everything was prepared. She had been written up for some sedative medication if she became aggressive at the revelation. Nurse Crisp had drafted in an extra two nursing assistants who were on standby should physical restraint become necessary.

Dr Winstanley looked uncharacteristically pensive as she walked in the bright sunlight to Cypress. She flicked her dog end into one of the shrubs underneath the office window.

Morning Shelley. You okay? Think we best not have hot drinks in there today in case she launches them at us. Maybe a few cold drinks?"

Shelley returned with a tray of cold drinks and a plate of biscuits. Jammy Dodgers and party biscuits. They seemed like an incongruous choice, but the stores were not due to be replenished until this afternoon, so these were all that were left.

The seating in the quiet room had been arranged by Dr Winstanley. She had placed the staff chairs by the door to facilitate a quick exit should Lara become violent.

The scene was set.

"Could you get her please, Shelley?" Dr Winstanley asked.

Lara was already walking towards the quiet room through the dormitory. Shelley smiled warmly at her. She did not smile back. "Hi Lara. The doctor is waiting for you."

Dr Winstanley gestured for Lara to sit down in the chair she had assigned as the least risky. Oh, the doctor is uncharacteristically nervous thought Shelley. She was sat forward in her chair, seemingly ready for flight. She noticed a blush on her chest; sunburn or nerves she wondered? Her voice lacked its usual modulation. Lara immediately picked up these nonverbal cues. Something was amiss. She must guard herself and be ready. She fixed her eyes on the doctor. The atmosphere was charged. Shelley wished she were anywhere but in this room. The initial fears she had on her first day about Lara's unpredictability had returned, and she felt her heart pounding and her stomach lurching. She recalled the scene in the bathroom with Nurse Slater, her stunned eyes gawping at the ceiling as her lifeblood seeped out around her. What if her complicity in Nurse Slater's death now put them both at risk? Her flight instinct was strong. Resisting the urge to run out of the room, she tried to focus on the snow scene in the picture above Lara's head.

"Lara," Dr Winstanley began. She gave a nervous cough as she tried to get the right tone in her voice.

"Lara, today is different. I do not have any tasks for you. I have news. Big news, that we hope will be good for you to hear but might also make you upset. I want you to try and relax. Shelley and I both care about you and want the best for you. I am going to assume you understand."

The doctor paused to take a sip of orange juice. Her mouth felt dry.

"We have been looking at your case notes since you came to Wellswood Lara. It has been a long, long time. Before either of us were born in fact."

Lara watched. Impatient. She wanted to shake the news out of her. What good news could she possibly have. The last good news she had received was when she was to leave Celyn to move into Nancy's cottage.

"We have found letters in your file. Letters that have helped us to understand your story."

Lara resisted the strongest urge to use her voice than she had in years. It felt like a growl she had to quieten. Her chest hurt.

"Lara, there were two letters in particular that led us to the truth."

The pain in Lara's chest intensified. The growl grew, occupying every bit of space in her thorax.

Shelley noted an increase in the rate of Lara's breathing and saw the rise and fall of her chest although her face remained impassive.

"The letters were from Dr Franklin. And from your mother."

Lara feared the growl might be released. She must control it.

"They both lied to you, Lara. About your baby? Your little girl?"

Dr Winstanley hesitated and waited for a reaction. She too observed the increase in Lara's breathing. And then took the biggest punt of her career. She left her seat and knelt before Lara.

Shelley was aghast. What on God's earth is she doing? Getting ready to intervene, she tried to garner inner strength to restrain Lara if she kicked off.

Doctor Winstanley held both of Lara's hands and dropped her voice to a honeyed whisper.

"Sweetie."

Shelley remembered the day when she had so unexpectedly used that word with her.

"Your baby did not die. She is very much alive. She is still in Landscove."

The quiet room had never been quieter. It held its breath. Dr Winstanley remained kneeling on the floor, as if in a silent prayer. Lara did not push her hands away. She stared at the doctor in her prostrate position. She briefly looked at Shelley as if to confirm the truth of this revelation. Shelley's face told her it was true. Her baby was alive? She needed more. Tell me more she wanted to scream. Instead, she let out a strangled noise. It was not the noise she had been expecting. It was louder and more pained than she had thought it would be. It caused the doctor to lurch backwards. Shelley went to help her up and they both stood expectantly. I need to see her. I must go to her now thought Lara. She stood up and made for the door. I need to see her. I have to go now. Now.

The two women parted to let her make her exit. Lara opened the door and pushed past the staff who were clustered at the door ready to spring into action. They had all heard the noise. Inhuman was the general consensus, when they discussed it later. Primal, guttural, inexplicable.

They looked to the doctor for direction.

"Hang fire guys. We will just wait in the wings. See which way she flies".

She took a cigarette from the carton and lit up with a slightly shaky hand. Nurse Crisp raised her eyebrows.

"Cut me a break, Crisp! I need this."

They all congregated in the foyer. Henty came through from the dayroom.

"The witch is dead," she said, and they all laughed in relief. The patients had all been saying it since Nurse Slater had died. Nobody knew who had said it first, but it had caught on.

"Sister Berry is going to love that!" Shelley said.

"Yep. If she ever comes back. Which I doubt" Dr Winstanley said cryptically.

Lara had still not emerged. Ten minutes had elapsed.

"Shall I go down to her room? Check out what she is doing?"

"Okay Shelley. We will hang back and will be right behind you. No heroics, just shout for help if you need us. Leave the door open."

Shelley walked down the dormitory towards Lara's side room. She knocked gently on the door and walked in. When Lara saw it was Shelley, she did not stop. She was brushing her hair. All her clothes were piled on the bed and Tiny Tears was laid on top of them all.

"Hey Lara, what's going on? Are you okay?"

Lara turned her navy gaze on her.

"My baby. I see my baby now".

She turned and carried on emptying drawers and putting the contents on her bed. She was looking for something. In the corner she found it. The doll's dummy. She picked it up and turned it over in her hands.

"Oh Lara. Your baby is all grown up now. Too old for a dummy."

Lara stared at Shelley incredulously. She put the dummy in the baby's mouth and handed the doll to Lara.

"Give it to Mary," she said.

Chapter 33

Lara carried her coat over her arm. She stuffed her hairbrush and toothbrush in the pockets. She needed to be ready. She looked behind her. That is all, she thought. She bowled down the dormitory. The staff were all gathered in the foyer where she had left them. She could not imagine why they were still there. She walked past them straight out of the double doors into the heat of the day. Bewildered, they all watched her go.

"We have got to stop her," Nurse Crisp said.

"We can't stop her. She is an informal patient now and has been for years. She could have left anytime she liked," Dr Winstanley replied.

"But she's vulnerable. She has not walked out of this hospital ever. She has no idea. She will get knocked over before she gets to Mallock High Street," countered Nurse Crisp.

"She wants to see her baby," Dr Winstanley said.

"What, are you just going to let her walk to Landscove?"

"No of course not. I am going to take her to see her baby. You are going to lend me your car. Shelley, you are coming with me. Nurse Crisp, you need to inform Mr Scott but give it half an hour. I don't want any knee jerk responses. And ring Dolly Lane. I have written her number in the back of her notes. Under next of kin."

Dumbly handing over the keys to her car, she nodded her agreement and started to write up the daily report. It would be a longer report than usual. Lara Demengel had a voice! She was mute but not dumb as had been believed for so long. It was the biggest revelation of her career. And confirmed her belief to always assume capacity.

Lara was walking briskly out of the gates when they caught up with her. She did not stop as the car slowed beside her.

Shelley spoke to her through the window while the doctor drove slowly alongside her.

"Lara. We are not taking you back to Cypress. We will take you to see Dolly."

Lara snapped her head towards Shelley who realised her mistake and the reason for her confusion.

"Your daughter. They called her Dolly. We will take you to her."

Considering her options, Lara stopped and looked at the car. The last time she had been in a car was 38 years ago, coming in through those gates. Shelley got out and opened the back door. Lara got in and slid across the seat. The seats were hot.

"Shelley, get in the back with her. I will need to keep the windows open to let some air in. Tell her everything we know about Dolly. Better tell her about Jack and Dylan too!"

Lara stared out of the window whilst Shelley told her about how they had found Dolly through Cally Newby. She told her that Dolly was a mum herself, and that she was a grandma to two fine looking boys, omitting the fact that they had been the object of some considerable mooning by both her and the doctor. Lara looked at

Shelley then and smiled, "Grandma." she echoed. Dr Winstanley caught Shelley's eye in the rear-view mirror and winked.; she had not heard Lara speak before.

She wondered how much language she had. She could not imagine how she had not used her voice for so long, tucked it up deep within herself. She could not know about the singing and soothing of the dolls; first those stolen moments with Mary Ryan's doll and more lately with her own.

She hoped that Nurse Crisp had managed to get hold of Dolly, and that she was home to answer the call. She did not want to imagine the scene if they arrived unannounced. All of her previous concerns about potential danger had dissipated. Lara was behaving like most people would if they discovered a child thought dead, was alive.

The doctor pulled into a garage. Lara looked agitated.

"I am just going to get us some cold drinks." She relaxed back into the seat, lifting the backs of her legs from the seats where they had become glued by the heat.

Back on the road, Dr Winstanley turned her head to her passengers. Not long now she announced.

Lara sat upright now as they entered Landscove. The Rose was still there, and the church. Memories came flooding back, she could not filter them. She pushed them away. My baby. See my baby.

Chapter 34

The doctor parked beside the lane that led to the beach and Dolly's.

"You okay to walk the rest of the way Lara? It's a bit tight for the car."

She answered by moving across towards the door.

"Here we are then, Lara. Almost there."

Like a homing pigeon Lara sped off down the lane. Shelley struggled to keep up with her as Dr Winstanley locked up the car and trotted down the lane after them. By the time they had caught up with her, Lara had passed the track to Dolly's and was walking towards the sea. She stopped and looked seaward. Dr Winstanley fumbled in her bag for a smoke. Shelley tried to catch her breath. Lara was smiling broadly. The sea was flat calm, shimmering like diamonds in the sunlight.

"Dolly's house is there."

The three women turned to look at it. Lara recognised it as the old fisherman's cottage. The cobbled front yard that housed nets and lobster pots had gone and the deck stood in its place. She had first met the Reverend Pinkerton there. She had been riding Solomon and had got off to collect shells.

A woman had risen from her chair on the deck and was looking at them. She covered her open mouth with her hand. She had been expecting them. A Nurse Crisp had rung ahead to alert her. Walking towards the deck, Lara did not tear her eyes away from Dolly. Almost breaking into a run, she made her way towards the five wooden steps up to the deck. She hesitated only for a moment before opening her arms wide. "My baby". Dolly walked slowly into her embrace and allowed herself to be enfolded in her mother's arms, the second time in 38 years.

Amazed, Dr Winstanley looked on. Her next concern was how it would finish. Lara would have to return to Wellswood tonight. Would she have to go back in an ambulance? Sedated like the first time she went in? She tried not to let that taint this monumental moment. Shelley tried without success to stem the flow of tears but it hardly mattered; nobody was paying any attention to her.

Dolly had been shocked to hear that the cautiously planned visit she had discussed with Dr Winstanley had taken such an unexpected turn. Jack was doing his shift at the Rose and Dylan was at his girlfriend's house. She had called Daniel to come home and be around should things take a sinister turn. She had fussed around the house, rearranging cushions and straightening out throws. Lunch. She must rustle up some food for her visitors. Her Birth Mother. She could barely believe she would clap eyes on her mother in the next hour. She had no idea what to expect. When she saw her on the beach with the doctor and Shelley, she knew immediately what she would look like in 20 years. Despite her shapeless nylon stretch dress, she could see an older version of herself. She noted how she looked an indeterminate age. She has less wrinkles than me she noted. And she almost sprinted up the beach. Dolly had been told she was mute so was taken aback when she called her "my baby". Lara's voice was raspy and quiet; like she had a terrible sore throat. It did not feel like she was in the arms of a stranger when she held her. She felt familiar. It felt completely natural. She hoped Tabitha would be looking down and approving this moment.

Lara stepped back to survey her daughter. She traced her face like a blind woman might, drawing her finger along her nose and the curve of her chin. She stroked her hair. She brushed her lip with her thumb. She was transfixed. Dolly stood and allowed her face to be analysed. Daniel appeared at the doorway. Like his wife, he was barefoot and wearing cut down denim jeans and a white T-shirt which showed off his athletic physique. Grabbing his hand and pulling him towards her, Dolly said, "This is Daniel. My husband."

Lara looked at him and made no response. Seemingly unfazed, he said how delighted he was to meet her and how pleased he was that she and Dolly could get to know each other. He suggested everyone sit whilst he got some lunch and drinks together. Lara remained standing until Dolly sat and beckoned her to come sit by her.

As the food came out, Shelley stiffened as she thought about Lara's lack of table manners; she ate like a savage. But Lara had a different agenda today. Preoccupied, she barely ate and did not cram the food like she usually did. Whilst it was not quite tea at the Ritz, it wasn't feeding time at the zoo either.

Shelley and Dr Winstanley said they would leave them to it for half an hour and take a stroll along the beach. This would give them time to think how they might negotiate a return to Wellswood. They both took off their shoes and walked in the shallows. Shelley longed to get in. It was hot and she felt uncomfortable. She had liked swimming as a child but had stopped going to the pool as her growing self-consciousness about her size had developed; not helped by her brothers by calling her Shelley Belly or The Fridge.

Four cigarettes later, they returned to the beach house where Lara and Dolly were bent over photos.

Dolly looked up. Within that half an hour, Lara and Dolly had made a bond, an invisible thread that connected them. Shelley thought apart from the terrible dress and hair that looked like it had been hacked by gardening shears, it was hard to believe Lara had been institutionalised for nearly 40 years. Just this morning, Lara had believed this woman, her baby, to be dead. Everyone at Wellswood had believed Lara to be mute and uncomprehending.

"I have agreed to come to Wellswood on Sunday. To visit. With the boys and Daniel. "

Seeing that Lara brooked no argument, Dr Winstanley mentally cancelled the ambulance and riot police and silently blessed Dolly.

"Can I use your phone please, Dolly? I just need to let the ward know we will be back later. And to return the car I practically stole!"

Within the hour, they were headed back to Wellswood. Clutching a photo of Dolly and the boys, Lara smiled all the way back.

Chapter 35

It was Shelley's last day of her placement on Cypress. She had two weeks annual leave and then two weeks back in school before she was launched onto Larch Villa, a male "high-grade ward". Nurse Crisp had readily agreed for her to pick up some extra shifts and finish off her case study.

"Have you told Lara you are moving on, Nurse Merrigan?"

"Should I?"

"Of course! Even if there is no outward sign of any attachment, you are the first nurse in years to pay her any positive attention."

"I was hoping to maintain some contact. Maybe keep visiting?"

"Oh Shelley," Nurse Crisp sighed heavily. "There will be a "Lara" on every ward you work in. You will soon lose interest. Don't make any promises that you are really unlikely to be able to keep. Best to manage your ending properly. Hard as that feels now."

Shelley could not envisage a time when she was not wholly consumed by Lara. Nurse Crisp could never know the ties that tied them. Or the lies that tied them, thought Shelley wryly.

"I have redone your Student Nurse report. Sister Berry clearly wanted to bury you! Shelley, don't ever be a sheep.

Remind yourself every day that this job is a privilege. Making their shit lives a bit brighter. Don't ever abuse this power. The patients are people. This is it for most of them. Until they close this hellhole down, which they will one day, we are the best chance they have for a better quality of life. I know about your reporting to Dr Winstanley. Oh, don't look so worried Shelley! I wish I had the balls to do the same. I am pretty confident Sister Berry will not return here. Between you and me, I am likely to be made up to ward sister."

"That is great news! But what have you heard about Sister Berry?"

"She is on "gardening leave". Suspended in other words. Pending an investigation into her gross misconduct. There are plenty of others crawling out of the woodwork ready to chuck the bitch under the bus. And hopefully Slater is in the pits of hell getting her just desserts. You did a brave thing."

She wished she felt brave. All she could think of were the times she had idled mutely and allowed these poor women to be hurt. She pictured Pammy, rocking backwards and forwards to try and comfort herself after been struck around the head. And Grace and the ladle, lying bleeding on the floor, with her dinner down her front. No, she did not feel brave. She felt it was a stain on her soul that no amount of Hail Mary's would remove. Lara was the brave one. Stopping Nurse Slater in her tracks. Rescuing Pammy. There was no dereliction of duty from Lara. Righteous anger.

"Lara's family? Do you think they will come today?"

"I hope so, Sister Crisp. Sounds good, do you think? Although I would be thinking about getting married with a name like Crisp!" joked Shelley.

"There is still time to change your report you know!"

Shelley went and knocked on Lara's door and waited before she went in. Her bed had been made neatly and her clothes folded neatly back in the drawers. She had left Tiny Tears with Mary, who was delighted with the new addition to her plastic family.

"Can I sit down, Lara?"

Lara shifted up on the bed to make space.

"Big day for you Lara. Your people coming to see you."

Lara investigated her lap and removed invisible specks of dirt from her dress.

"Would you like me to do something with your hair? Maybe a bit of lipstick?" Lara shook her head.

"Lara. You know I am a student nurse, right? It means I was only ever here for 3 months."

Nonchalantly, Lara picked up her hairbrush and started to brush her hair. Dust motes danced in the shaft of sunlight coming through the window, agitated now with each stroke of the brush.

"I am so, so happy you have found Dolly. And you have two grandsons! I could not be more made up for you."

Lara carried on brushing her hair.

"Lara. One more thing. What happened in the bathroom? With Nurse Slater? I will never breathe a word. I haven't even told Dr Winstanley. And I will not. Ever. What you did? I wish I had been brave enough to do it."

Lara gently placed the hairbrush on the chest of drawers in a slow and deliberate motion. She did not look at Shelley. But for the briefest of moments that

Shelley sometimes doubted happened, she leant into her and placed her head against her side. She then stood up abruptly and Shelley recognised the nonverbal cue; she had been dismissed.

At 2pm, a green Vauxhall viva pulled into one of the parking bays in the hospital grounds. It was another hot day, but with a gentle breeze bringing with it some respite from the searing sunlight. Jack and Dylan stretched their legs. They had argued on the way about the lyrics to Metal Guru; Jack had insisted it was Nelly Balloo. He enjoyed winding Dylan up; he was so easy. In reality, they were fiercely loyal to each other, and woe betide anyone who tried to drive a wedge between them. The joking stopped abruptly as they drove through the grounds of Wellswood. This was a whole other parallel universe they had no idea existed. There was a woman rocking backwards and forwards flapping her hands in front of her face. Jack was mesmerised, she had the same rhythm as the rocking horse at the doctor's surgery in Landscove.

"Don't stare, Jack," admonished his mother. There was a giant-sized pram being pushed by a nurse. Jack peered inside. He could not distinguish whether it was a man or a woman, a child or an adult. The head was impossibly large with a tangle of limbs, the legs scissored over each other and hands held in tight claws. He was fascinated. This is where his grandmother had been kept for nearly 40 years. He had adored Tabitha, his Nanny Goat as he had always called her. They both did, and missed her acutely. Both quietened now by the enormity of the occasion. Meeting their lunatic Granny.

Some of the patients were sat outside. Jack felt like it was some kind of circus exhibition. He had never seen anything like it before. He had not foreseen this, the noise, the distortions of humanity. How could nature go so horribly wrong? And when they entered Cypress, the smell almost made him gag. The windows and doors were all open, but it was not enough to blow away the smell of raw humanity that lingered in the fabric of the building. He wanted a fag desperately but fancied his parents did not know, thinking naively they had been hoodwinked by the polo mints.

The family gathered in the foyer and were soon met by Shelley. Nurse Crisp came out of the office and greeted them warmly.

"I have set up the quiet room for you all, if you feel like you want us close by. Or you are free of course to go for a walk in the grounds. They are quite beautiful this time of year and it is a lovely day. I will be right here in the office so please feel free to ask me any questions you might have."

"I think we will start off here and play it by ear. Thank you so much," Dolly said, trying to quell the revulsion she felt for Cypress, the smell and the noise. She could not fight it; she was shocked and appalled. Dolly had concocted a picture in her mind of genteel men and women reclining in wicker chaise lounges being tended to by doctors and nurses. She knew that was a fantasy, but the grim reality shook her to her core. All the women were wearing the same dress her mother had worn last week, albeit in slightly different colours. The same hacked hair and heavy brown shoes. The men they had seen all seemed to be wearing the same trousers, half-mast with an elasticated top. She felt inexplicably depressed at the sight. She thought of her idyllic life on what she considered to be Cornwall's best beach, her faithful, handsome husband and her dazzling, amusing boys. She silently gave thanks again to Tabitha for her rescue. What kind of monsters could have left Lara to rot in this hellhole?

Tea had been thoughtfully laid out in the quiet room. Dolly noticed there were china cups and saucers for them and a blue plastic cup and saucer. She looked questioningly at Janet who bought in the tray.

"Patients' cups," she offered by way of explanation.

"Here she is," Nurse Crisp said, opening the door for Lara. "I will leave you to it."

Lara stepped inside the door and waited to be alone with "her people" as Shelley had called them. Her first visitors since she was brought here strapped to a trolley. And here was Dolly, the baby that was ripped from her arms, leaving her bereft with a deep chasm of grief. Her Nancy, and then her baby. She looked up at these two boys, identical except for the small mark under the right eye on one of them, which she also bore. They looked a bit like Theo and Bertie; she thought fleetingly of the brothers she had barely thought of over the years.

She looked lost, Dolly thought. Catching her mood, Dolly took charge of the situation. She introduced Jack and Dylan and suggested they all sit down for tea. Lara did not move. She stood with her back to the door, surveying the scene before her. Daniel bristled with the tension. Had they made a wrong decision bringing the boys here? To see this strange woman with her vacant stare and strange stage whispers? He could never tell Dolly he had lain awake the night after Lara's visit in a quandary. What if Dolly went mad suddenly? Or if she had passed on the family malady to the boys? Dylan was sensitive at times. What if it were a sign he would go mental and have to be locked up. He wished Dolly was still blissfully ignorant of her parentage. That this misfortune, as he saw it, had not come knocking to potentially upend their happy life.

Lara stepped towards Dylan now. She looked at him intently. She held his head in her hands and bent down. She pressed her lips to his head and took in a deep inhalation. He smelled of summer. She gave him the slightest of smiles and did the same to Jack. He smelled of the beach and cigarettes. She stroked his cheek. She then opened her arms to Dolly who stepped into her embrace. Daniel, she ignored. She was not sure of him. He was too comfortable, too sure of himself. He reminded her of some of the boys from the village who had put themselves inside her, not all gently. She would watch and wait. He would need to prove himself.

Dolly was not sure what to call Lara. It felt wrong to call her Mum somehow; Tabitha had been her Mum. She didn't want to alienate or cause her upset by calling her Lara either. It became too difficult to keep avoiding calling her anything. Clearing her throat, she tried it out.

"Mother. I have brought you a few gifts." She handed a bag to Lara. She had not had a gift since Nancy had given her the last Wesley, a tiny ball of fluff, all eyes and a wet nose.

She unraveled a dress. It was a linen turquoise shift. Very elegant. Lara had not seen anything like it before. The fashions of the 1930's were starkly different.

"There's more," Dolly said, and pulled out a sheer white scarf in a slippery material. Lara hated them. She remembered Nancy forcing her into her Sunday best ready for a rare visitation from Loveday. But she knew she would wear it to please Dolly. She would wear it until it became threadbare to please her girl.

"Thank you" she said in her raspy voice, folding them back into the bag.

"You will need shoes too," Dolly said, looking at Lara's clodhoppers. "Next time."

The boys relaxed although neither could eat or drink anything. The smells had managed to meld inside their nostrils. Dylan feared he would never eat again. Both were pleasantly surprised by Lara. She did not look deformed in any way. In fact, Jack said on the way home, she would be a very good-looking older woman if you discounted the mad clothes and dodgy hairstyle. And the weird staring and crazy talking malarkey.

All too quickly for Lara, an hour had elapsed and Daniel announced it was time to go. Her heart sank. When, if ever, would she see them again? But, like a bandage around her heart, Jack kissed her cheek and said, "Goodbye Grandma. See you soon." Dylan followed suit. Lara felt like she had swallowed the sun, a bright yellow ball of happiness replacing the dark hollow of grief she had felt for so long. Dolly kissed her mother lightly on the cheek.

"We will be back soon. I promise."

With a light spirit, Lara walked down the dormitory to her side room. Mary was fussing her doll, smoothing down her hair with a hand that was beginning to claw up with arthritis.

"How is baby today, Mary?"

"Happy girl today Lara. "

Lara lay on her bed to relive the afternoon, on repeat.

Chapter 36

The car was like a furnace after standing in the glare of the sun. Dylan was ready to slake his thirst with a bottle of Lucozade, only to find it was now warm. They were just pulling out of the gates of Wellswood when Dolly said six words that would change their lives.

"I cannot leave her in there."

Daniel felt his heart plummet in his chest, like a lift with a severed cable chord. In that moment, he sensed a seismic shift in his universe. He wished their lives could go back to a time when Lara Demengel was just a scribble of ink on Dolly's birth certificate. Daniel's knuckles tightened around the steering wheel.

"She doesn't belong in there."

"It's her home Dolly. Has been for nearly 40 years."

"But did you see the other women" Some of them were like vegetables. Just sat there making noises on beanbags."

"Dolly, she has lived there almost her whole life. She is happy."

"All she did was have a baby, Daniel. That is not a crime. She has been locked up all this time. What about my father, whoever he is? Where is his punishment?"

"Dolly, darling," he said, softening his voice. "The baby couldn't have been all that was wrong. Sweetheart, she is odd. Backward. You must see that."

"Dr Winstanley said it is because she has been institutionalised for so long".

"She was institutionalised because she is subnormal."

And there it was. He had said it. The word lingered in the car all the way back to Landscove. A frosty atmosphere pervaded the boiling car.

Daniel felt unsettled. Their marriage had been unusually harmonious. He always felt blessed when he heard his mates talk about their mardy wives. Dolly was even tempered and slow to anger. She was undemanding. Maybe because Daniel did everything in his power to make sure she was happy. He adored her and felt lucky every day to be the one singled out for her affections. The four of them were a cohesive unit, impenetrable and close. Or so he had thought.

Dolly stormed up the steps to the deck and flung the door open. Two minutes later she flew out again, with her costume on and a towel slung over her shoulder. The three boys looked after her.

"Going for a rage swim then? Dylan said, as she stomped towards the water.

"Grandma is pretty weird obviously. But kind of cool too. Not too many of my mates have a grandparent in a loony bin."

Daniel snapped. "That's it. I don't want to hear any more about that bloody woman."

Dylan shrugged. The boys slunk away. It would soon be the Sunday night Top 40 on the radio. They usually crowded around the transistor on the beach with their mates from the village. They would take a blanket down and have an evening swim or a surf if the waves were favourable. Now they were eighteen, they had progressed from cans of Coke to a few beers. Their house, and their parents, were normally by far the coolest. But not tonight. Perhaps tonight they would avoid the beach house and make a campfire down on the beach. Give them a little time to make up.

When they returned to the house at eleven pm, Dolly was already in bed. Daniel was on the deck with a glass tumbler of whiskey, his dark mood obvious from ten paces. He drained his glass when he saw the boys. "I'm turning in. Kill the lights and lock up when you go to bed."

Daniel and Dolly each kept resolutely to their side of the bed. There were three feet and a sea of resentment between them. Daniel accidentally touched Dolly's leg: she recoiled as if she had been touched by an electric eel.

The icy standoff lasted five days. Dolly had to buckle in order to ask Daniel if he would drive her to Mallock on Sunday, or should she ask her brother? She had never lamented not taking driving lessons until now. She detested her reliance on Daniel and resolved to pass her test.

"I will take you."

Chapter 37

The boys both had an extra shift at The Rose on Sunday. There were "Emmet's" aplenty, according to Todd, so it was all hands on deck until September. Then Landscove and the rest of Cornwall was returned to the locals, and they could all breathe a sigh of relief. The summer was a double-edged sword. The tourist pound helped to support the villagers through the winter and there was some fresh meat for the lads. Always a holiday romance to be had. The outsiders would flood in, all pale goose-bumped flesh, screeching as they waded into the shallows. The Landscove lads were tanned by May and used to the Baltic temperatures, they surfed and swam with grace. An intoxicating sight for the city dwellers. Even the plainest villager managed to hook up with a holidaymaker by the time summer had passed.

Dolly had brought some sandals for Lara. Rose gold with crisscross straps and the smallest of heels. She was not sure Lara would be able to walk in them after being used to wearing the industrial type shoes favoured by the inhabitants of Cypress. She had also brought her some toiletries; a pretty shell soap on a rope and some Fenjal bubble bath, her favourites. Dolly had made a driftwood photo frame and placed a family photo of them all from last Christmas in the frame. A box of rosewater and lemon Turkish Delight completed the package. Dolly wanted to make up for the privations of her incarceration with a few luxuries.

Dolly put the gifts on the back seat as they started the journey once again.

They had progressed from silence to icy politeness.

"Could you open your window a little wider please?"

"Could you pass me an extra strong mint, please. They are in the glove compartment."

This visit seemed easier, Dolly thought. Lara seemed less guarded, but she continued to ignore Daniel. She was wearing her new dress and scarf. If she had a decent haircut and a blow dry, she would look like an elegant older woman. Dolly passed her the sandals. She took off her clumpy shoes and put them on, turning her feet this way and that to admire them. She inhaled the fragrance of her soap on a rope and the bubble bath and gave a small sigh of pleasure. She ran her hand across the photo, feeling the intricate knots of the driftwood. Dolly had to open the box of Turkish Delight; Lara had no idea what it was. She popped a rosewater cube in her mouth, leaving a powdery residue around her lips. She made an appreciative noise; she hadn't tasted anything like it before. Dolly found a hanky in her bag and passed it to Lara.

"How about a walk? I would love to look around the grounds," Dolly suggested. Lara got up readily and led the way.

"The League of Friends run a little tearoom at the weekends. Opposite Laburnum ward. If you fancy a decent cuppa," Nurse Crisp had advised them.

The grounds were beautiful in the late summer sun, the trees heavy in leaf. Dolly saw that each villa had been named after a nearby tree; sycamore, walnut, furze. The League of Friends' shop was run by volunteers from Mallock. Ken Loftus' wife, Sheila, made the teas. Today they had some fruit cake slices and a few Kit Kats housed under a plastic dome. They bought some teas and sat outside on the white plastic chairs, convivially laid out for an al fresco tea. Despite being outside, Dolly could hear noises emanating from the nearby villas. She was convinced again of an urgency to get her mother out of this madhouse. If only Daniel would yield. They had agreed to put on a show of a united front in front of Lara, but it was unnecessary. Lara was oblivious to anything outside of the orbit of Dolly; she could not tear her eyes away from her face. She looked at her in wonder. The greatest miracle of all time, her baby returned to her. Whole and perfectly lovely.

They heard a low whistle. "Look at you, Lara Demengel. You look nice." Dolly looked up to see a man with Down's syndrome grinning widely at Lara. She turned away, but not before Dolly saw the faintest of smiles and a little flush of her cheeks. The man walked off, humming a little tune Dolly recognised as something they played on Sunday Night at the London Palladium.

Dolly raised her eyebrows at Lara. Too early for teasing she assessed correctly. After dropping Lara off at Cypress, Dolly promised to come again next Sunday. Looking pointedly at Daniel, she added, "If I can get a lift, that is." She watched Lara walk down the dormitory. If she had come back in five minutes, she would have seen the discarded sandals, dress and scarf on the bed and Lara back in her regulation shoes and dress. She buffed up the photo frame with her scarf and placed it carefully on her little chest of drawers. She hid everything else in her drawers. Even though things on the ward had improved since the spectre of Berry and Slater had gone, Henty still could not help herself but steal. Anything missing on the ward was usually found secreted in her drawers. "Beryl Henderson is a kleptomaniac," she had heard Sister Berry telling a student nurse years ago. No surprise there; what she hadn't known was her first name was Beryl. Everyone called her Henty. Lots of the patients had nick names. She knew hers was Creeping Jesus. She thought she would be amazed if they knew the nicknames she had for them over the years!

Like a thunderstorm after a heatwave, the first rumble was Dolly. She had never felt so out of control. In that moment, she looked at Daniel's rigid profile and hated him. How could he be so selfish? What if it was his mother locked up like that? Would he leave her in there to languish? Daniel's hands gripped the steering wheel and his knuckles whitened. His lips were drawn back across his teeth. He swerved the car into a lay-by and got out of the car, slamming the door fiercely. He raked his hands through his hair and paced up and down. He was so enraged he did not know what to do. He felt his marriage falling apart on this roadside. They had never argued like this. He cursed Lara. He cursed those bloody meddlers, Dr Winstanley and Shelley, for coming into their perfect world and destroying it.

"What do you want from me, Dolly? To have that bloody weirdo in my house? I would never sleep soundly in my bed again."

It was worse than he imagined.

"Yes, Daniel. That is exactly what I want."

Chapter 38

Shelley got a call from Dr Winstanley. She had started her second placement on Larch Villa. Nurse Crisp had given her a good ward report and she was feeling much more "nursey" after a further two weeks in block. The male ward seemed so much more straightforward. Far fewer staff dynamics. The charge nurse rarely left the office so Shelley and the nursing assistant did all the work. It was a mystery what he did in the office all day. There was very little to do in the way of administration beyond compiling the off duty, writing the daily report and ordering the stores. He would dust himself off to do the medication round. A little foray in his drawer would have thrown up the answer, a quart of Bell's whiskey. No wonder his mood improved as the shift progressed. He was lazy, but benign, so it suited Shelley.

"Shelley, can you come over tonight? Gray is making a spag bol and I have a good bottle of red. I need to talk to you. Away from here preferably."

This would be Shelley's second visit to the doctor's. Much to Julie's amazement and amusement.

"Ooh fraternising with the doctor now!" she'd mock.

Julie could not imagine what they had in common. Shelley had not expected a friendship either, failing to recognise that the doctor probably felt as alien as she did in amongst the Cornish born and bred. "Incomers," they were referred to. The Winstanley's had a large semi on the outskirts of Mallock. Her husband Gray, short for Graham Shelley presumed, had extended a warm welcome to her. He had a strong West country accent. They had apparently met at a party in Bristol "centuries ago". Dr Winstanley loved that Gray had no propensity for anything medical. He loved numbers and worked as an accountant. He also loved model railways, the loft completely given over to a complex network of railway tracks and trains, including a rack and pinion engine that climbed up a small fiberglass hill. Vix rolled her eyes at the mention of it, but clearly did not mind in the slightest. Their son, James, was polite but aloof and keen to absent himself from his parents at the earliest opportunity.

"If you call me Doctor Winstanley one more time Shelley, I swear I will have to headbutt you!" Shelley laughed and forced herself to call her Vix. It seemed easier in her own home where she was spread out on her Habitat brown cord settees. And after imbibing a good deal of red wine. Shelley had never drunk red wine before. Tastes like sour Ribena, she thought. She was shocked when she saw her stained teeth and lips in the bathroom cabinet mirror and swore to stick to white wine in the future.

But here she was again, red wine in hand, chatting, while Gray threw a strand of spaghetti at the tiles behind the cooker. Five more minutes he announced.

"Ideal, time for another fag," Vix said, cigarette smoke mingling with the steam from the boiling pot.

"Any chance James will stop studying the Littlewoods catalogue lingerie section long enough to join us?" Vix asked casually. Shelley snorted red wine down her chin. Gray laughed.

"You would think he would be more cheerful the time he spends up in his room. I will give him a shout."

Shelley was amazed by the division of labour. Gray seemed more than comfortable in the kitchen. Her Da had never as much boiled an egg. When her Ma had a hysterectomy, all the other Ma's brought food around; colcannon and the like. As if Da himself had undergone the surgery. They both left all the dishes piled up in the kitchen after too: Gray retreating to the loft and his trains and Vix into the lounge to carry on with her bottle of red, a pack of Marlboro lights and an ashtray.

Refreshing their glasses, Vix said "I have been asked to report my findings to the GNC. "

Shelley looked blank for a moment. "The General Nursing Council," Vix continued, "About Sister Berry. She is strenuously denying any abuse of course."

Shelley paled.

"Don't worry Shelley. There are enough other people who are more than willing to dob her in. It would appear she is not as well connected as she liked to think. I almost feel sorry for that sap Scott. He is all sweaty and anxious at the sound of her name. And your tutor Devonish is saying he was unaware of any cruelty or negligence on Cypress. Otherwise he never would have allowed his student nurses on the ward. Lame."

"It's true I never saw her directly hit any of the patients herself."

"She might as well have, Shelley. She did nothing to protect those women. Nothing. And by all accounts she loved every minute of her reign of terror. Lapped it up.

Wound Slater up like a toy and watched her play out her evil games. I think she was probably worse than Nurse Slater. Her duplicity. At least Slater never pretended to be anything she wasn't. Evil old bitch."

Talking about them took a shine off the evening. She felt the familiar shame at her impotence at not taking robust action against them. And once again, tortured by the memory of Lara and her strangled NOOOOO, as she brought Nurse Slater's campaign of torture to an abrupt end.

"But anyway, that's not the reason I asked you over. It's this," she said, thrusting a letter at her. "It's from Dolly."

Dear Dr Winstanley

First of all, I want to thank you for all your efforts in reuniting me and Lara. My Mother! It still sounds so weird to say the word. As you know, I have been visiting her on Cypress. I am very shocked by the conditions she is being kept in. I know the staff make a lot of effort to try and make it more homely, but it feels so wrong that she is in there. I know she is probably a bit slow in her thinking and her speech is odd, but she does not belong there. I know you said that the effects of the institution are as damaging as what was wrong originally. Could those effects be reversed? Like if she lived in a normal family. Could she ever function outside Wellswood?

All she did wrong was to have a baby? Daniel has his doubts she could ever function outside the confines of the hospital. He worries she could be dangerous and pose a risk to our family.

There is enough room for her in the beach house. There is a whole annex which the twins hardly use now as they are rarely home these days.

It feels like the right thing to do. I would be grateful for your opinion.

Yours Sincerely,
Dolly Lane.

"Well! I didn't see that coming," Shelley said.

"You know Shelley, places like Wellswood won't be around forever. There will be a big push to close the old institutions up and to provide care in the community."

"Oh, but surely not in our lifetime," laughed Shelley, "I don't want to go through all this training for nothing."

"Mark my words. It will happen. Apart from anything else, most of these hospitals are built on prime land. They will sell them all off for sure. It will be highly lucrative. A property developer's dream! Then the powers that be will pass it off as progress in how we provide care for the mentally ill and the mentally handicapped. Writing is on the wall, Shell."

"Vix, Lara couldn't lead a normal life outside Wellswood. Could she?"

"Well, I think it would be a huge adjustment. But with careful management of the transition? Yep. I see no reason why not."

"What about her potential for violence? What Daniel said? Could he have a point?" She thought of her own accountability. Her silence over the death of Nurse Slater. What if someone else crossed her? And she had kept silent. She would be partially responsible.

"She is burnt out Shelley. She is as dangerous as you or I. Like a snake with the venom removed. I am confident she will be fine. But we will need your help. You want a project? Some brownie points for your training?"

"What?" Shelley asked.

"Extend the scope of your case study on Lara. Part two if you like. Follow her journey out of Wellswood into the community. Join me for all the case conferences. And then help Lara with the transition. And work with the family to help reintegrate her back into her community. As well as massively helping me out, it won't do your career any harm either. What do you say?"

Shelley relished a legitimate reason to stay involved with Lara. She raised her glass and nodded her agreement. She could scarcely imagine Lara leaving Wellswood. Was it possible to undo almost forty years of institutionalisation and reintegrate back into society?

Chapter 39

Daniel wondered where this stubbornness had come from. He had never seen Dolly so resolute. Since the eruption in the lay-by, they had at least dropped the cold war, as Daniel thought of it. He was pretty sure she was fully prepared to have Lara live with them, even if it meant that their marriage was dissolved. He could never have foreseen any external threat to their happiness. He knew that if he wanted to keep Dolly, he would have to bend to her will. He was, however, resolute he would put up a fight. He would raise doubts about her safety around the boys. He had tried to dissuade her by saying she would be alienated by the village, lose all her friends. Nobody would call by anymore, once they had satisfied their curiosity about this odd creature roaming around, staring and talking in a strangled whisper.

Dolly said she didn't give a rat's arse about anyone else's opinion. She said the doctor would have told her if she was dangerous or a risk to anyone. Only then would she consider changing her mind. Meanwhile, she busied herself preparing the annex for Lara. The boys, pragmatic as always, said whatever Mum decided to do was okay by them. They had both taken to Lara; they thought despite her peculiarities that she was sweet and endearing, like some kind of stray pet they were considering adopting. They had happily helped Dolly get rid of their boyhood detritus. Sensing defeat, Daniel helped Dolly paint the annex in the palest of yellows. He made a beautiful driftwood bed which Dolly dressed with a patchwork quilt, hand stitched by Tabitha. She created a gallery wall of light brush seascapes and pretty jugs she would fill with wildflowers. A large picture window provided an ocean view with white muslin curtains fluttering in the sea breeze and thick, damask curtains in a sandy hue providing a much needed second layer against the wintry storms. Dolly looked back to admire her handiwork. Pretty. Really pretty. She went down the two steps into the bathroom. Daniel had re-enameled the cast iron bath that had originally been in the cottage. It was far deeper than modern baths and Dolly had been delighted to have repurposed it. She had also repainted an old washstand with a marble top. With a large blue and white jug and bowl, it looked perfect. A large venetian mirror reflected the room in all its glory. Some hand-crafted soaps and a new bale of fluffy white towels completed the look. Daniel saw it all and wished it were for someone else. The reality of Lara being here, and not leaving, left him feeling cold. But here they were, well down the path of no return. The die was cast.

Chapter 40

Shelley had been granted permission by the school of nursing to undertake this bespoke piece of work. There was a degree of excitement about it. Nobody left Wellswood except via the morgue. Mr Devonish was keen to endorse this development in a bid to deflect attention away from his ill-advised friendship with the now maligned Sister Berry. Before anything else, they had to ask Lara if she wanted to go. All her adult life she had been cocooned within these walls. She may well have developed a sense of security about being insulated from the outside world. Leaving may be a step too far, despite having no obvious attachments to either staff or fellow patients.

Back in the quiet room, Dr Winstanley and Shelley once again summoned Lara. By now, there was no furtiveness and Lara was at ease with them both. She looked expectantly at the doctor.

"L   ted things are working out so
well   And things on Cypress seem to
be g   ce the staff have changed?"

L   ked up a biscuit and examined
it be

'   ever thought about leaving
Cyp

Lara looked up abruptly, a bewildered look on her face.

"I mean Wellswood," she clarified.

"Every day," Lara said. Clear as a bell. Dr Winstanley laid out the plan. Dolly wanted her to move into the beach house. There would be a process of course. There were lots of hoops to jump through to make sure it was the right decision for all of them. They had to help Dolly to understand and dispense her medication just for starters.

Lara shook her head vehemently. She stood up and indicated with her head for them to follow her. She went outside and snaked her way by the hedgerows and shrubs that grew outside the villa. Outside her bedroom window, she pointed to a mountain of discarded plastic capsules and large white tablets.

"How long?" the Doctor said open mouthed.

"Forever," she replied.

The three women looked at the pile of discarded medication. It was Doctor Winstanley who was first to snort with laughter. Then Shelley and finally Lara who hadn't laughed like that for years. She could barely remember laughing so hard. Till tears came. A vision of Nancy, soaked to the skin and fuming, suddenly came back to her. Was it possible that that was the last time she had laughed like this? It felt good. She felt suddenly light at the possibilities ahead. Would she remember how to swim? Maybe she could ride again if she weren't too old. To have the chance to be a mother, a grandmother. Could this be true? Getting out of here. It felt like a dream. She could scarcely believe it.

"So that's one less task for Dolly, for sure," Shelley said, the laughter beginning to subside.

The planning began in earnest. There were case conferences to plan aftercare. The GP from Landscove had attended and had agreed to oversee any general medical needs but Dr Winstanley would remain her responsible medical practitioner. She would see Lara in outpatients every six months as standard, more frequently if required. Readmission would be straightforward and could be arranged quickly should the home situation break down. Like a no quibble return on faulty goods, Shelley thought. Shelley had been to assess the home. She had wanted to move in herself. The annex of the beach house was like something out of a lifestyle magazine.

They had established that Lara was not on any prescribed medication currently. Any risks to others were now assessed to be negligible, the assault on Nurse Treloar ancient history. Shelley had shifted uncomfortably in her seat and studied her pen closely when the issue of risk was raised in one of the discharge planning meetings. She hoped to God that she was right; Lara had reacted after years of provocation by Nurse Slater. And that she did not pose a risk to the public at large. That she would not take umbrage at random strangers and willfully attack them. It pricked her conscience, but it was too late to suddenly come clean. Her concealment would signify the end of her career. Maybe even her liberty. No. She must remain silent. The moment for transparency had gone. Her and Lara were forever entwined by that moment. Mostly, Shelley was able to justify her silence to herself. But in moments like this, she had the tiniest doubt that mushroomed into a pervasive anxiety that she had got it spectacularly wrong. She remembered the ferocity of that push. She had meant business. Then she reminded herself that she had been protecting Pammy. It was not a spontaneous act of violence without any antecedent. No. It would be okay she soothed herself. Shelley came to; everyone was packing up their paperwork. The case conference was over. Shelley had completely missed the last bit.

"Sorry Vix. I zoned out at the end there. What's going on? "

"Trial weekend next weekend. We are dropping her off and Dolly and Daniel will bring her back on Sunday evening. And you, my friend, are on standby if the shit hits the fan! So, no getting pissed!"

The drive to Landscove had become familiar now. The high hedges bordering narrow lanes that gave tantalising glimpses of ocean. The autumn was now giving way to winter. The trees had been stripped bare and stood starkly against a gunmetal grey sky. Lara and Shelley sat in companionable silence in the back seat as the scenery scudded past, both lost in thought. Dolly had told the hospital not to bother packing anything. She had everything Lara needed for the weekend.

"You okay, Lara?" enquired Shelley.

After a moment's thought, she nodded her head. "Very okay Shelley."

It gave Shelley a flash of warmth when she used her name. Her life would be the poorer once Lara had gone, she suddenly acknowledged to herself.

Daniel, Dolly, Jack and Dylan were all ready and waiting on the deck. There were rainclouds forming over the horizon. A portent of doom, thought Daniel, fixing his face in a welcome. If he wanted Dolly, he had to endure this. The waves were fierce, real dumpers. There was a storm brewing for sure. It matched his mood, dark and unsettled.

Here she was. The antithesis of everything desirable in his life. Dressed in what looked like a German greatcoat. He was dismayed that this day had finally arrived and his life, so envied by others, was about to be trashed. He held back as his wife and sons greeted her so warmly. He mumbled his greeting to her. It had started to spit. By the time they were all in the door, the heavens opened, the clouds opened up, and the rain fell. "Proper stair rods," Dolly said, as they blessed their timing. A large fire was already lit, taking the chill off the air. The inglenook fireplace ran the entire length of the lounge wall. The fire basket was heavily laden with gnarled, dried, driftwood and a woody smell permeated the lounge. Tea was laid out in preparation.

"Would you like to see your room?" Dolly asked. "Whilst the tea is brewing?" Lara followed Dolly into her room. She took in every detail. It reminded her of seeing Nancy's cottage for the first time. The beautiful simplicity after the stuffy grandeur of Celyn. And now the contrast of this elegant room after her cell in Cypress.

Dolly waited anxiously for her response as Lara drank it in.

"Do you like it?" she asked.

"Love it. Thank you Dolly," she said.

"Oh, thank goodness for that! I really want you to feel settled and at home here. Really I do."

Vix and Shelley left them. They were soaked by the time they got into the car. "Oh what I wouldn't give to be a fly on the wall, Shelley!"

"I hope it will be okay. Not sure Daniel's cup was overflowing, to be honest. But the boys were sweet with her, weren't they?"

"Daniel might be the proverbial fly in the ointment. We will find out soon enough!"

Dolly had made pasties for lunch. She had a flair for cooking; she seemed to have an almost instinctive ability to marry flavours, and everything she made tasted good. She had laid the table in the kitchen. She hoped Lara would feel more comfortable in there than in the formal dining room. They only really used it for guests and Christmas. The kitchen was warm from the AGA cooker and cosy. Dolly had painted a large dresser in an antique cream and had an eclectic mix of pretty china she had accumulated over the years. They sat around the large, scrubbed, pitch pine table that was set with knives and forks.

"Wow, Mum, looks great, thanks!" Dylan said as he cut his pasty in half. A column of steam funneled towards the ceiling.

"Watch out, they're hot," Dolly warned.

Lara watched as they all wielded a knife and fork. She had not used them since leaving Celyn. Nancy had turned a blind eye to her dispensing with eating utensils. She had used a spoon in Cypress and her hands during her time on Beech.

She picked up her pasty with her hand a nibbled the braided pastry edge. Seeing her discomfort, Dylan abandoned his knife and fork and took a big bite into his pasty. They all followed suit. All except Daniel. Lara ravished hers quickly, wiping crumbs with the back of her hand. Dylan and Jack found it amusing of course.

"So, we are all to start eating like a pack of wolves, are we?" Daniel hissed over the washing up.

"Give her a chance Daniel."

"Well, I don't want the boys to think they have a license to start eating like bloody savages."

"They won't. Keep your voice down."

The rain had passed, although the clouds hung over the beach with a promise of more to come.

"Can I go walk?" Lara asked.

"Of course. I will come with you. I will get you one of my coats. And some wellingtons."

Kitted out against the weather, they walked the length of the beach. Dolly looped her arm in Lara's who hugged it tightly to her side. The spray from the waves soaked them and Lara laughed.

"Did you ever come here before? Before?"

Lara nodded and broke off the arm link. She made towards the hilly path that cut through the sand dunes to the cove at Celyn. She stopped at the top of the hill and looked down at the cove. As familiar to her once as her own hand. The bracelet of black rocks. The curve of the shoreline. The scrubby grass at the base of the dunes. Where Nancy had lain, like a fallen statue. The last time she had been there. Just before Dolly was born. She turned away, her eyes smarting in the wind that was picking up. Dolly held her hand out and Lara gripped it gratefully.

"Nancy." Lara said aloud." Can I see Nancy?"

Dolly looked bewildered. She had no idea who Nancy was.

"Dead. She is dead." Lara said by way of explanation.

"Oh, I see. Shall we go in the morning? Is she in the churchyard at St. Bede's? We can try and find her and take flowers?"

"Yes. Yes please."

Dolly drew Lara a deep bath. After asking if she wanted bubbles, she threw in a cap full of Fenjal bath oil. The smell drifted in the steam and Lara inhaled deeply. Dolly said to call her if she needed anything and left her to it. She put her toe in. Hot water. The type you had to submerge in slowly. Hot enough to leave your skin red. Delicious. She sank under the bubbles, allowing the water to minister to every part of her. She felt her hair fan out around her head. She sat up with her nose barely out of the water, like a truffling seal, until the water started to cool. She reluctantly heaved herself out of the tub and wrapped herself in a towel so soft she would be surprised if it would dry her. Dolly had laid out a white cotton nightdress with a tiny floral detail around the neckline. She had also draped a pink quilted dressing gown and some slippers for her. She had not skimped on any detail for her comfort. Toothbrush, hairbrush, a bedside glass of water, covered with a dainty lace cloth. She had even laid out some magazines. Family Circle. Good Housekeeping. Cosmopolitan. Lara liked the smell of the glossy pages. She looked curiously at the photos. Women looking nothing like they had in her day. For the past forty years she had only seen women in a uniform of some description; either nurse or patient. Fascinated, she flicked through the pages. Young women with glittery blue eye shadow graced the pages. Hair flicked like the wings of a dove, sweeping away from their faces. She looked across at her own reflection. She had never been one to think much about her appearance, even less so since she had been in Wellswood. But now she picked up her heavy hanks of her hair in her hand. No longer black but shot through with grey now. She looked like she was from another era. She would ask Dolly about a haircut.

Lara slept fitfully. The bed felt like a giant marshmallow enveloping her. The thick curtains muffled the sound of the wind and the roar of the waves. But she felt restless. Memories crowded her mind now. Highly polished boots on the sand. Wet lips like liver, enveloping her mouth, leaving her face damp. Solomon's bowed head eating grass. Wesley running in and out of the surf. A thud. Nancy's body slumped on the rough ground like a felled tree. Her own scream. Holding Nancy as the warmth left her body. The darkening sky. The cold seeping into her bones. She sat up now in bed, trying to sweep away the dark thoughts. She tried to remember Theo's face. All she could conjure up was an amalgam of Jack and Dylan's faces. The physical similarity was obvious, except Theo's features were always distorted by his revulsion of her. Her whole family was a blur. Milla obviously looked like a mirror image of herself. Emmeline was a wisp of a memory. Her mother she remembered well. Stiff dark blonde curls framing her face, wreathed in disapproval. Bertie and her father she could barely recall. Her father was like a dark shadow creeping around the corridors of Celyn. She wondered, for the first time, what had happened to them all. She had forced herself to stop thinking about them when it was perfectly clear she had been long forgotten in Wellswood.

Lara eventually slept. She momentarily had no idea where she was when Dolly came into her bedroom, bringing her a cup of tea.

"I didn't mean to wake you." she said apologetically.

Lara sat up in bed and rubbed her eye, removing a crust of sleep in the process. She smiled her thanks. She had not had a cup of tea in bed for forty years!

"Did you sleep well? I hope the storm didn't keep you awake. It was wild! But it has blown over now. It is a beautiful day. My favourite kind of day. Dry, crisp and cold. Now after breakfast, I am going to have a little dip. In the sea! Daniel thinks I am crazy" she said, inwardly balking at the term crazy. Lara did not seem to have noticed.

"I go every day. You can come and watch if you like. And then we can go and find Nancy in the churchyard."

After breakfast, they headed to the sea. The tide was high. Dolly slipped off her coat. She had her costume on underneath. She waded in until she was waist height and then she slipped beneath the waves. She turned and waved at Lara who waved back and smiled. Dolly had told her she usually swam out towards Celyn's cove and back. Lara walked alongside as Dolly swam. Her stroke was smooth and fast. Lara longed to join her; she wondered if she would still be able to swim. The waves looked like smooth watery mountains as Dolly rose and dropped in between the waves. She tried to remember the feeling of the cold water slapping against her face, the salty taste in her mouth, the rippled sand on the seabed, the hermit crabs burrowing away from her as she put her head in and propelled herself forward like a windmill. She wished she had a costume. She did not want to alarm Dolly with nakedness. Dolly came out, skin puce and cold, like refrigerated meat. Smiling, she daubed herself dry with her towel and pulled her coat tightly around her.

"Best start to the day, Mum."

The word hung between them. She was sure Tabitha would not object, and the look on Lara's face blew away any sense of disloyalty. She smiled broadly.

After Dolly was dressed, she gave Daniel a kiss on the forehead. The first sign of a thaw he thought.

"Keep an eye on the dinner won't you. Dylan is bringing Katie apparently. We shan't be too long."

They walked towards the village. A very diminished congregation were leaving after the morning service. Dolly was a Christmas, weddings and funeral type of churchgoer. Nothing against God in particular, she had just never really given it much thought. Tabitha had been an avid fan of church. They had a sign above the dining table. "Christ is the unseen guest at every meal, the unseen listener at every conversation." She liked the idea, but hadn't had any occasion in her life so dismal as to call out to Him.

"So. Do you remember anything else about Nancy? Her surname?"

"Cooke. Died when you came."

Dolly had no idea what she meant until they found it. A simple headstone, no frills, much like Nancy. There was a browning bouquet. Louise had kept up her mother's tradition of laying flowers on Nancy's grave after Cally had passed. Lara bent down, removed the old flowers and replaced them with the ones they had bought from the mini store, the only shop open on a Sunday in Landscove. They were cheap and wilting but it was all they had. With great reverence, Lara lay the flowers on her grave. She touched the headstone, feeling the cold stone beneath her fingers.

Nancy Cooke

Rest in Eternal peace

Fell asleep 29th October 1937.

Until we meet again.

The day before my birthday thought Dolly.

"My best mum," she said to Dolly, "The best "

Dolly was mystified. She had thought her mother's name was Loveday. She thought she might be confused. So, she took her to her family plot, not knowing what her reaction might be.

There she saw the roll call of her family's deaths.

Charles Demengel

Bertrand Demengel.

Loveday Franklin

Emmeline nee Demengel

Did that mean Theo and Milla were still alive? Or buried somewhere else?

Lara felt detached. She felt complete indifference to her dead parents and siblings. But she trailed back to Nancy's grave and tried to make out the words again.

"Shall I read it to you?"

Lara nodded and committed the words to memory so she would know when she came back.

They walked back towards the beach house. As they walked across the deck, the smell of a roasting lamb hit them. Dolly busied herself with the final preparations as Lara hung up her coat in the cloakroom. The twins burst in, bringing a gust of cold air with them. Lara smiled at them and resisted the urge to enfold them in her arms.

"Grandma. This is Katie. My girlfriend."

"Hello Katie" she said. They all hid their surprise at this appropriate transaction.

There was a moment of tension as dinner was served. Dolly had tactfully cut Lara's meat into more manageable sizes without making it obvious she had cut up her food. Lara picked up her dessert spoon and skillfully ate her dinner with this. She had forgotten food tasted like this! She had to force herself to slow down, reminding herself there was plenty and none of these people were likely to steal her dinner. Everyone chatted in a relaxed way and passed the potatoes, or extra mint sauce and gravy in an unhurried way. Lara looked at this handsome family, her people, and felt content. This memory would help her survive the rest of her time in Wellswood. Just two more weeks, then she was back here again for a week. All too quickly, it was time for her to go back to Wellswood.

After dropping Lara back at Wellswood, Daniel returned home. Thank God she had gone. He wished it hadn't gone so well. Dolly was full of it. Did you hear how clearly she said hello to Katie? How she is with the boys? Oh Daniel, you should have seen her at Nancy's grave. There was genuine emotion on her face. I know this is the right thing to do. It will all work out; I just know it. For the first time in months, she allowed him close to her in bed. He held on to her like a life raft, his gratitude to be the one man in Landscove to be allowed to touch this beautiful creature flooding back. We all have our cross to bear, he thought grimly as his ardour cooled. Maybe she will die prematurely like the rest of her damn family he thought; hating himself for having such dark thoughts, but hating Lara more.

Chapter 41

It was harder than ever before to be back in Cypress. The smell she had become immune to assaulted her afresh as she walked back towards her side room. The food was barely palatable after home cooked food. It bought to mind her first few months when she was 17, when everything in Wellswood was new. The noise; humanity at its most raw. Nakedness, cruelty, the odd kindness. The total lack of privacy or dignity. People watching you poo. Or if they missed the event, asking about it and recording it in their pointless books. The next two weeks until she went back to the beach house felt longer than any other time. She had some things she wanted to do which would fill some time.

Ken Loftus. She wanted him to know she was sorry she had scared him that day on the coach. And to say thank you for bringing some faith back to people. He had smiled at her warmly as he did all the patients. And his wife, Sheila, who worked in the League of Friend's shop. She always gave Lara a smoke if she was passing when she was out the back having a fag break. Lara would never demean herself by going to the office to ask the staff for a smoke; she did not want them to have the power over her. But she would cajole other patients when she was out in the grounds.

And she wanted to see David. To say goodbye.

David had been there in 1937, pushing his silver dinner cart, when Lara was wheeled into Cherry ward, strapped down on a trolley surrounded by bullish looking men. They were mocking her, laughing as she fought against her restraints. She had a livid looking eye, and she was covered in blood. In his palsied voice, he told them to leave her alone. One of them laughed and pushed David into a bush. Humiliated, he cursed the men. It took time to get up. His body did not do what he wanted it to do. He knew he was ineffectual against them. Anger burned within him; he hated the injustice and the abuse of power. By the dried blood between her legs, he figured this was another mother who had their young torn from them. David had been at Wellswood since he was 18 when his mother had died. When David was eighteen months old, the doctor had told his mother he was a spastic and advised her to put him away and forget about him. She found she was unable to unhook from the child. She would stare defiantly at onlookers who looked at her with pity as he drooled onto the large handkerchief she tied around his neck. David was a revelation to his mother, who discovered at age five that he was able to read better than his older brothers. It was painfully slow but there was no doubt that his intellect was intact. He was cruelly trapped in his own body. When she passed away, his brothers were unable to care for him. They had their own families and couldn't afford a dependent sibling. They did visit though, as they had promised their mother they would.

David saw Lara again a few months later. The black eye had gone, and she was now dressed in a shapeless brown dress that looked like it had been made from burlap. Her hair had been butchered; he suspected to cut out where it had been matted with blood. She was a good deal thinner than when she was being wheeled onto Cherry. No longer tanned, her sallow skin was drawn taut across her protruding cheekbones. What in God's name have they done to her, he lamented.

She was like a graceful imp, barely there, insubstantial, as if she might disappear. She was slipping between the row of imposing trees that bordered the perimeter fence. He saw she was trailing a hand along the fence. Maybe looking for an exit that was not there? He knew, he had done the same six years ago.

He had not meant to startle her. He wished more than ever before he could alert her to his presence by using his voice. He knew it never sounded like it did when he spoke in his head. Instead, he lurched into her path with his mangled body. She halted in front of him, and recoiled like a cat, ready to pounce. He tried to put his hands up to demonstrate a conciliatory stance. Lara balled up a fist, ready to launch when recognition crossed her face. She remembered his plaintive pleas to the henchmen who bought her in to Wellswood to leave her alone. She recalled his defeated body, sprawled in a bush. This was not a foe, she uncurled her fist, and waited.

"Smoke?" She did not understand him at first until he falteringly handed her a cigarette. Still suspicious, but gasping for a smoke, she gingerly took it from him. He handed her a box of Swan Vestas.

She lit her cigarette and handed the matches back, her face never leaving his.

Each word an effort, he told her his name was David and he lived on Almond ward. And that he worked with the porters, bringing the food to the villas. He said that he had seen her on her first day. He said he was sorry she had been hurt by those men; that he could not help her. Lara listened attentively and became accustomed to the rhythm of his voice and understood him.

Then, with a twisted agony he asked,

"Did you have a baby?"

She hesitated. Tears sprung to her eyes.

"My baby is dead. "

David staggered towards her. He meant only to hold her, to comfort her. Lara lay down on the grass. Impassively, she lifted her dress. David looked away, mortified. He had never before seen so much of a woman. He wanted to unsee her lying like that before him. He could not foist himself onto the fragile creature before him with his clumsy limbs. This was far away from his agenda.

"No," he stammered. Lara jumped up quickly, smoothing her dress down. Her face was wreathed in confusion. She could not fathom what he wanted from her.

"I want to be your friend."

And so he was. For the next 38 years he sought her out whenever he could. When he heard she was locked up on Beech he would stand outside the dayroom windows across the yard where they were fenced off. Lara saw him every day and was comforted by his presence. When she was transferred back to Cypress, she would meet him away from the prying eyes of staff. She did not say much. She accepted his cigarettes gratefully and never offered herself to him again. His sweet love for her had been the thing that sustained her all these years. He often had a small gift for her. A chocolate bar or a few biscuits. Once he gave her a small kingfisher brooch he had found in the hedgerow. It was most gratefully received, along with a few smokes, sometimes just butts he had foraged and managed to roll in cigarette papers.

She had not been able to tell him about her weekend with Dolly. He had been so happy for her when she told him Dolly had been found. He was so pleased she would be leaving Wellswood soon and had promised to visit her in Landscove. Lara so wanted her family to meet David, her saviour for all these years.

She scoured the grounds for him but could not find him. She went down to the kitchens; he might be there early today getting his trolley prepared in readiness for lunch. He had slowed down over the past eighteen months; the trolley proving more cumbersome than before. His legs were more buckled than in his youth. His trolley was easy to spot. It had David painted on the side in a vivid red. Today, his trolley was being pushed by a porter she had not seen before, He was not a patient. She started to feel uneasy; there was no such thing as a holiday in Wellswood. You were either working, or dead. Despite her worries, she felt unable to ask the porter where David was.

Shelley. She would help. She quickly made her way to Furze. Shelley was on her third placement now. Furze villa was tucked away near the staff social club. Lara walked through the doors and stood outside the nursing office and waited. A young nurse came out of the clinical room holding a steel kidney dish with a syringe in it. She nearly dropped it when she saw Lara standing there.

"Oh shit! Sorry! You made me jump."

She waited for Lara to say something. Lara looked at the kidney dish and debated with herself whether to say something.

"Shelley," she whispered.

"Nurse Merrigan? Shelley Merrigan?"

Lara nodded.

"Right on in there," she nodded with her head towards the dayroom as she disappeared off down the corridor.

Shelley was carefully doing the drug round, reading to herself aloud from the medication card in front of her before popping Epilim out from its silver blister pack. "200, 400, 600mg."

Lara tugged her sleeve and Shelley spun around. She checked herself; how unexpected it was to see Lara here. She had no idea how she could have found her but remembered she had told Lara her next ward would be Furze.

"Well, what brings you here Lara?" she said with obvious pleasure.

"David."

"Huh?"

It was not enough. Lara knew she would have to elaborate.

"David Girling."

"Is he a patient Lara?"

"My friend. Almond." Shelley suddenly realised it was the David she had seen around. Cerebral palsy David. Closing the medication trolley, she indicated for

Lara to follow her into the office. She rang Almond on the internal phone. She soon established that David was on Cherry, the sick ward. He had been there since the weekend.

"He is very poorly Lara," Shelley said.

Lara looked stricken. Shelley rang Dr Winstanley whose office was located in the corridor next to Cherry.

"Send her over and I will take her to him."

They were both astounded that Lara described anyone as a friend. It was thought she was an isolate, with no emotional connections to anyone within Wellswood, or indeed, outside.

Dr Winstanley was outside waiting for Lara.

"He is very sick Lara. If we had known, we would have told you before."

Lara was agitated now, she needed to see him for herself. She followed the doctor down the row of beds. She heard the low hiss of the oxygen tank. He had a mask clamped over his nose and mouth that fogged as he exhaled. He was propped up on three pillows. His body looked like a broken puppet under the white sheet that was neatly folded across his naked chest. Lara's heart hurt, he looked so pathetic. He was asleep. Dr Winstanley called his name tenderly. He opened his eyes slowly.

"There is someone here to see you, David."

David looked beyond the doctor and saw Lara. His arm jerked as he tried to remove his mask. Lara put her hand out to stop him.

"Don't David."

Lara sat on the chair the doctor had dragged from the other side of the ward. She placed a hand on Lara's shoulder.

"Stay as long as you want sweetie," she said. "I will phone Sister Crisp and tell her you are here, so they don't get the search party out."

"I will be right here," she promised, as she went to phone home and tell Gray she would be late tonight.

She made the call to Gray and then rang Furze.

"Shell, can you bloody well believe it? What else is Lara keeping from us?"

"I know! I couldn't believe it when she turned up on Furze. How is he?"

"Her timing is impeccable. He will not last the night, poor guy. He has exceeded expectations though. I cannot imagine anyone expected him to reach 62. His body has just folded. I rang his brother this lunchtime to tell him he is gravely ill. He couldn't come; he has health issues of his own. He asked me to let him know when the inevitable happened. But surprise, surprise, he will not die alone. I am staggered, Shelley, I don't mind telling you. That woman is full of surprises! Pop over if you can when your shift finishes. I am going to stay on. Crispy knows she is here."

Lara stroked David's hands as he drifted in and out of sleep. She wished her will could make him well. She longed for his breathing to pick up pace again. For him to fumble around in his shirt pocket and hand her a painstakingly rolled cigarette. To hear him guffaw with laughter at her impressions of Sister Berry. And to listen intently to her whispered confession that she had pushed Nurse Slater into the wall and killed her. His dark brown eyes looking at her so softly as he cuffed his drool with his shirt sleeve. She knew he was leaving her.

At least he had been spared the pain of her leaving him alone in this place.

His breathing was barely discernible now. A nurse came in, lifted his wrist, and took his pulse. She held her fob watch as she watched the rise and fall of his chest. She went and summoned the doctor. His respirations are down to five per minute she heard her tell Dr Winstanley.

"He doesn't have long now Lara," she said quietly.

She walked away. Lara stood and leant into him, muffling her mouth into his ear, she sang faintly.

"Half a pound of tuppeny rice, half a pound of treacle."

She stroked his head gently and kissed his forehead. His transition from this life to the next was almost seamless. He was, and then he was not.

Lara allowed herself to be held by Shelley as she soothed her in her arms.

"It's okay, it's okay Lara."

As his body began to cool and mottle, Dr Winstanley indicated to Shelley that it was time for Lara to go back.

Lara brooked no argument. She bent to kiss him one more time, his forehead marbling now.

"Goodbye, my friend," she said quietly. Then she walked into the cold night and back to Cypress.

Chapter 42

For a brief, joyous moment when she woke up, Lara forgot that David was dead. Like a freight train, the grief hit her afresh. Nancy's death had heralded a catastrophic sequence of events for her. She had worn the pain of her loss like a cloak, dark and cold. And now David. She worried that his death was a harbinger of doom; a bad omen that her life would once again take a downward turn. Until she had found Dolly, Nancy and David were the only authentic connections in her life. Those trusted few that she had let penetrate her sturdy wall of suspicion. She could not be here in Wellswood without him. She could not contemplate leaving here for a week and then returning. It would be torturous. The move to Dolly's had to be permanent. Lara could not grasp the protracted process of transition. It made no sense to drag it out. She just wanted to be at the beach house in Landscove. With Dolly and the boys. Daniel she would have to tolerate as part of the deal.

She would have liked to have stayed in bed for the next two weeks, licking her wounds and focusing on her grief. There was a knock on her door. It was Sister Crisp, encouraging her to get up and have some breakfast. She was not unkind, Lara had noticed. She realised she had not eaten since the previous morning.

The discus of solidified porridge would give her some energy to face the day. She needed to speak to Dr Winstanley and speed this up; she needed to be with her family and start the next chapter of her life, whatever was left to her.

After her breakfast, Lara slipped out and made her way to Cherry. The grass was encrusted with frost now and crunched beneath her footsteps. She met Dr Winstanley who was on her way out to do ward rounds. She noted Lara looked pale and tired. She was most surprised to see she looked as if she had wrestled with grief through the night; another contradictory manifestation of this woman assumed to have little in the way of emotional warmth. Apparently, no staff had been aware of the friendship between Lara and David. Their connection had been conducted completely under the radar. The staff usually knew of this kind of liaison, so they could take prophylactic steps against pregnancy. Many of the women had been sterilized without their knowledge or consent.

Taking her coat off, Dr Winstanley led the way to her office. With effort, she opened the sash window the four inches it could before being jammed by a nail. She would need to speak to estates; this window was getting stiffer. Lara looked at the cigarette packet longingly.

"You want one?" she asked, surprised.

Lara gestured yes and took one gratefully. Wait till I tell Shelley this one, she thought, as she watched Lara inhale like a pro.

Dr Winstanley offered no opening gambit. She knew by now Lara would not venture over to her without a clear rationale. She waited for Lara to speak.

"I have to go. Now. And not come back."

Dr Winstanley pondered how succinctly Lara had made her needs known in under 10 words. She thought she would match this.

"I will see what I can do."

By 11am the next morning, Daniel and Dolly were outside Cypress to take Lara home for the last time. Shelley and Dr Winstanley were already there to facilitate her departure. As good as her word, Dr Winstanley had expedited her discharge with a caveat of immediate readmission should things at the beach house become unmanageable.

Dolly was completely agreeable, especially after hearing about the loss of David. It made little sense to Dolly to prolong the agony; it was either going to work, or it was going to fail. A further delay would not negate that possibility.

"It's just not tenable for her to stay in there, Daniel."

Daniel had gone straight to The Rose and got more drunk than he ever had before. By the end of the night, everyone knew Lara fucking Demengel was coming back. The name meant nothing to most, but a few of the older men looked startled and had scuttled home to their families.

Yet here he was, walking towards Cypress for the last time, to pick up this woman, his mother-in-law. He could not believe that a few short months ago, she had been nothing but a name on a piece of paper. And here she was, about to come and live in his house; his home, he corrected himself. With his family. The damn woman did not even look at him. He hoped beyond hope she would do something reprehensible that would see her swiftly and unceremoniously returned to Wellswood. This is where she belonged. A subnormal woman in a hospital for subnormals. Safe. Out of the way of decent people. Out of my life.

Lara had extraordinarily little to pack. The turquoise dress, white scarf and rose gold sandals were folded around the framed photo of Dolly and the boys. She handed them to Daniel at his behest. She went into the dayroom. "Bohemian Rhapsody" was at full volume on the radio. Pammy was sitting in her chair, smiling widely and rocking herself to and fro in time with the music. Toothless, she reminded Lara of a dolphin. Lara bent down and kissed her forehead. She whispered in her ear "The witch is dead. Goodbye Pammy." Pammy scrambled in the air until she found Lara's hand and squeezed it tight.

In the foyer, a farewell committee had gathered. Henty, Gracie, Lilly, Olivia and Eva were saying goodbye in their own ways. Lara looked over their heads back towards the dormitory and the bathroom.

"Okay, Mum, are you ready? Have you got everything?"

Suddenly, Lara seemed reluctant to leave. Daniel allowed himself a brief window of hope. Great. She does not want to leave after all. His fantasy was dashed by the appearance of Mary.

"Oh, Mary."

The two women embraced. Mary stroked Lara's cheek before kissing it.

"Goodbye Lara. God bless."

"Can go now," Lara said. Before climbing into the car, she turned to look at Dr Winstanley and Shelley. She took each of their hands in hers. "Thank you."

The car drove towards the next chapter of her life. Had she looked behind her, she would have seen Shelley and Dr Winstanley trying, and failing, to hold back their tears.

Chapter 43

Christmas preparations were underway in earnest at the beach house. Dolly felt light in spirit. The first two weeks of Lara being at home could not have been smoother. Lara had seemed happy to be there. She had already established a routine, something the doctor had predicted she would do; to replicate the rigid order in Wellswood. There had been a moment of amazement too. Dolly had been baking. Lara had been sitting at the table keeping her company and watching with a keen interest.

"Can I help?"

Dolly had stood back in astonishment as Lara picked up the ball of pastry. She lifted it to her nose and inhaled. Then she threw it down onto the table and threw some flour over it before rolling it expertly. She laughed and said "Nancy" by way of explanation. She had a real knack, Dolly discovered, for adding just the right herb or spice. They stood and cooked and baked companionably. Dolly could not have predicted this in a million years. She glowed from the inside.

One of the routines Lara had developed was lone walking along the shore every night before she retired. She loved the freedom of getting up and pacing up and down the beach, the roar of the sea drowning out all other thoughts. She would conjure up happy memories of David and of Nancy. She felt complete here with Dolly, Dylan and Jack. Even Katie, who was a regular guest at the beach house. There was a growing buzz of excitement about Christmas. The tree was already up, the lights twinkling in the dark evenings.

Christmas at Wellswood had passed like every other. Nurse Slater moaning she had to be there, looking after "you disgusting bitches", while the rest of the world celebrated at home with their families. There would be some festive treats ordered from the stores by the staff which did not leave the office. The Christmas dinner tasted like every other meal, bland and miserable. David usually tried to give her a little something special, usually what he had foraged from the grounds. Otherwise, it was devoid of any festive cheer.

Lara longed to go in the ocean. Dolly went in every day like clockwork. If it were "too lively", she would make her way to a deep tidal rock pool that would allow her to dunk as she called it, although she could only do a few strokes from one end to the next. Lara was not sure if she would remember how to swim. Once her own refuge, she now felt anxious that her body would have forgotten how to navigate the waves, how to propel herself forward and slice through the water the way Dolly did.

Daniel had developed his own routines. He was avoiding coming home. He was spending longer and longer at work and going straight to The Rose after work. He had always enjoyed the odd drink, but it was never something habitual. He had always felt there was something sad about propping up the bar in The Rose, night after night. He had always been eager to go home, to see his Dolly and the boys. Until the interloper came. His bitterness towards Lara had intensified. Before long, Daniel was confiding his distaste for his mother-in-law to Stacey, as she poured him another whiskey and Coke in The Rose. She was a great listener. She loved to hear about the potential demise of his perfect marriage to Dolly. She had a penchant for the older man and sought to exploit her advantage over Dolly. She knew that compared to Dolly, she was unrefined and raw. But she also knew aggrieved husbands overlooked this when she was able to soothe them, sweet talk all their troubles away momentarily. Daniel would be the biggest prize she had snared. He was handsome and had lots of money. She would love to winkle him away from his family. She brushed aside any niggling remorse she might feel about the twins. She was angry that they had both rebuffed her advances towards them when they first started working at The Rose. She was sure she could make Daniel notice her other charms aside from pouring drinks and listening to his complaints about Lara, and how Dolly no longer had time for him.

"Operation seduction" she said out loud into the chipped mirror above her sink, as she applied even more make up than usual. She made her lips like an oil slick with her Coty lip gloss. She fashioned her eyelashes into spikes with some clumpy mascara and tried to give more body to her thin hair with some vicious backcombing. She wore the most micro skirt she could find and a tight t-shirt and sprayed herself liberally with Charlie. He would notice her, she was determined. He did not smoke she had noted, so she chewed gum relentlessly to disguise the smell of Benson and Hedges on her breath.

"Oh, bloody hell. Who is the new victim?" sighed Todd, the landlord, when he whiffed her coming behind the bar for her shift.

"Never you mind," she smirked smugly. She eagerly watched the door. At six thirty, the door swung open, and Daniel entered. With a saccharine smile she leant across the bar.

"The usual, Dan?" she enquired unnecessarily, already pouring his whiskey. In an instant, Todd identified her prey.

"You've got no chance!" he side whispered.

"Just you wait and see," she smiled, ready to give Daniel her most sympathetic ear and eager to insidiously drip feed some toxic offerings of her own about Dolly and her disloyalty.

Daniel had gone home briefly to get a clean shirt. He had spilled coffee down the front. Dolly and Lara were sitting around the table. Dolly was showing Lara some old photos and she barely looked up as Daniel came in. "Your dinner is in the warming oven, Daniel" she had said as an aside.

"I have already eaten," he lied, planning a bag of chips. He was angry; the food smelled good.

He had had a chat with some of the old faces that frequented The Rose, but he gravitated towards where he felt the most sympathy was to be found. The men didn't really go beyond "ah they are all the same lad, have another drink". But Stacey really seemed to get it, she was a good listener and seemed to care about how difficult this all was for him. He knew her reputation of being a little tart of course. Dolly had called her a home wrecker after a good friend's husband had fallen for her obvious charms. Stacey had told the wife she was having an affair with her husband. Dolly's friend kicked him out and he moved into Stacey's little bedsit. The big romance had fizzled a few weeks after the secret was out. It seemed the thrill of the illicit was what Stacey craved. He had gone home begging to be forgiven, tail between his legs.

By 10.30, Daniel had lost the power of coherent speech. The bell for last orders had been rung.

"Time, gentlemen, please!" shouted Todd.

Daniel straightened himself up from where he had been slumped over the bar. He listed sideways and fell over a bar stool.

"Oh, come on, tiger," Stacey giggled as she wedged herself under his arm to help him stand straight. "Let's get you out of here."

Outside, the cold air caught him out and he swayed backwards, the wall breaking his fall. His head swam. His mouth filled with a sour liquid, and he was soon relieving his stomach of its contents on to the pavement. Stacey soothed him and rubbed his back. Her face blurred in and out of focus. Suddenly, Daniel put his hands behind her head and drew her in roughly, kissing her slick mouth. Her tongue darted in and out of his mouth with a vigour that surprised him. He did not care that he smelled of vomit. He was enthralled by the newness of her, her cheap perfume, the taste of cigarettes and chewing gum. He had only ever known Dolly in an intimate way, always making love to her with something close to reverence, something of a spiritual cleaving together of flesh. He grabbed her arm tightly, breathing heavily now as he was taken over by a primal need to overcome her. The carpark. He was in a high state of arousal. Stacey knew her victory was in sight. He was a bit rougher than she imagined; she did not care. In moments, he would be forever tied to her in some way. She would have one over on that spoiled bitch, Dolly and those boys who fancied themselves God's gifts to women.

He was steering her now towards the carpark and beer garden when headlights halted them. A car stopped and Jack got out.

Extricating his father from a dismayed Stacey, Jack grabbed his arm.

"Get in the car, Dad. I'm taking you home."

Furious, Stacey stamped her foot. Daniel, sobered a little by the sight of his son, got into the car with no complaint. Later he would see what a close call he had had. A few minutes with Stacey would be like finding a fiver and losing a million quid. He would have lost everything. The memory of her caused bile to rise in his throat, the cloying perfume, the fetid tobacco breath.

Dolly was in bed. The house was quiet. Jack guided Daniel to the kitchen.

"I will make you some coffee," he said, putting on the kettle.

"Is my dinner still in the warmer?"

Jack donned some oven gloves and placed his meal before him. Daniel registered he was famished; his chips from earlier now decorating the pavement outside The Rose. His passion had subsided; now he worried what Jack had seen. He started to ask Jack, who put his hand out to halt him.

"Dad, I don't want to know. She is a wrong 'un. Please, please give her a wide berth. Mum would never get over it, you know that." More quietly he added. "Neither would me or Dylan."

He left his dad to finish his meal and went to bed; he had an early start serving breakfast at The Rose in the morning.

Daniel needed some air. He wanted to clear his head and sober up before he slid into the bed next to his wife. He could still taste cigarettes and kept getting whiffs of perfume. Shit, he would have to put his shirt in the wash. He wondered how he could do that without raising suspicion; he had never used the washing machine before. Damn, he wasn't even sure how to.

He walked towards the water's edge. The wind had picked up and the waves were more than lively, as Dolly would call them. They were huge and fierce, thumping down angrily on the shoreline with a savage backwash. He relived his evening, culminating in his near miss with Stacey. He would have to tell Dolly before Stacey flaunted that nugget before her. He wondered if he might have been able to stop himself had Jack not appeared. He honestly assessed that likelihood as being the same as stopping a raging bull mid charge.

The sea looked inky under a pale moon. "I must still be drunk," Daniel mused, as he thought he saw a shadowy figure shifting closer to him. Blinking to try and focus on this apparition, he gasped as he realised this was no figment of his imagination. Someone else was out here. As the figure drew closer, he recognised her. Lara. The author and creator of all this doom. He had a brief fantasy of strangling her and letting the ocean take her. He imagined how Dolly would come back to him as he provided her with comfort over her loss. He could be the hero once again, the head of the family, holding all things together. He longed to see the warmth back in Dolly's eyes when she looked at him, instead of the disappointment that had now taken up residence. He stood rigid now, so fixed on her that he did not see the wave that swamped him and sucked him off the beach. He was pitched into a black nothingness of water, inhaling a lungful of briny water. He could not tell which way was up, as he was tossed in the waves. He hit his head on the bottom of the seabed. He flailed his arms around as blind panic gripped him. The cold water stiffened his limbs as he slowly surrendered himself to his fate. He was going to die tonight. A just punishment for his betrayal of his Dolly. The struggle leaving him, he felt a hand fumbling under his chin. The hand now getting a purchase, he was pulled above the waves and was able to take in a breath. Coughing and spluttering, he was vaguely aware of being held as a body swam beneath him. The waves continued to pound over both of them, but he was being held firmly and they were moving as one, he hoped, towards the shore. Dolly, he thought. My Dolly is saving me. He knew of nobody else brave enough to risk their own life to save his. He was flooded with gratitude. He would spend the rest of his life making it up to her. Never again would he complain about Lara. He would be the man she needed again.

They reached the beach. He was pulled up by his shirt out of danger. He spewed for the second time that night, salty water disappearing into the sand. As soon as she knew he was out of danger, Lara said, "I get Dolly," and ran towards the beach house to wake his wife.

Chapter 44

Daniel could not do enough for Lara. He had completely revised his opinion of her. He was full of gratitude and was now her chief cheerleader. That night had changed everything. By the summer of 1976, he could not relate to the Daniel who had any reservations about her. She was an oddity for sure, but she was fiercely protective of the family, and she loved them passionately. Dolly blossomed further through her care for Lara; her insistence on making sure she tried to make up for all her lost years in Wellswood. She had gone with her to the hairdressers after much persuasion to have her hair cut into flattering layers that framed her face. She wanted to go to the cinema, so they did. They cooked together and Lara now joined Dolly in her daily swim. Her fears were unfounded: after a few months she could swim as skillfully as she ever did, much to the astonishment of her family. Dylan and Jack were immensely proud of her prowess in the water. And Daniel told anyone who would listen how Lara had saved him from a watery grave.

Lara went regularly to Nancy's grave. She would tell her about her life and her family as she ripped out any weeds that dared to sprout in between visits. In the beach house garden, she had planted a rose bush in memory of David, which she tended with love. She wished he could have seen her now, that they could have walked along the beach together, shown off her little family.

At the end of the summer, Lara told Dolly she would like to visit Celyn. She had swum around to the cove a few times but said she wanted to see it, just once.

It had been a scorcher of a summer, the hottest on record. Even the newspapers were talking about it. "June, flaming June," the headlines of the Sun newspaper proclaimed. The grass was a scrubby brown; there was a ban on hosepipes so everything was dying. Cracks had appeared in the tarmac on the road. Lara was so relieved to be beside the sea, to dip in and find relief in the deep cooling water. She remembered the torture of her years in Wellswood, particularly when she was locked up in Beech. The sun streaming through the large windows made the ward like a hothouse, with no relief from a through draft. The stench, the noise.

"Okay Mum, are you ready for this?" Lara nodded, already feeling the heat of the sun warm her up after their morning swim. They had decided to take the car; the heatwave making them more lethargic than usual.

"It will be okay once we get going," Dolly said, opening all the windows.

By car the journey to Celyn was only a few minutes. The car turned into the gravel driveway, the stones crunching under the wheels and throwing up dust clouds where it was so dry.

Dolly parked. She left the windows open.

"It will feel like an oven when we get back in else" she explained.

Lara stood and looked at Celyn. She made no move to go in. Instead, she turned and said to Dolly she wanted to go this way. Dolly wondered why she was moving away from the main house. She hesitated outside the lodge that sold ice cream and teas. Lara walked right in and straight into the back room. "Hey, you can't go in there," the young girl, scooping vanilla ice cream into a cone said.

"I'll get her," Dolly said and followed Lara into the back room. The range was still there, blackened but pristine. No longer in use, Lara thought. The deep recessed window seats were the same. The flagged floor, the notch in the lintel. But the warmth had gone. Opening a door now to the back bedroom, the room where she had laboured and given birth to the tiny baby. It now housed boxes of crisps and crates of Coca Cola and Fanta. In the doorway, someone was calling for her to come. Her breathing quickened as the memories of the past flooded through her mind. She felt the tremors coursing through her as she tried to shake off the images that threatened to assault her now. Her mother and Dr Franklin, plotting in hushed tones about her fate. Cally Newby skittering around, trying to stop gawping at her and the baby. The dreadful absence of Nancy. Tabitha, looking shell shocked, but going through the motions of trying to clean up the debris of childbirth. The arms pulling the baby from her. The feeling of powerlessness. The punch in the face, the taste of blood in her mouth. The pains in her tummy, the aftershocks of labour. And the worst memory of all - the fading cries of her little girl as she was dragged away towards Wellswood.

Lara turned as she heard Dolly call her again.

A shaft of light fell and pooled on the flagged floor. She walked through it, like walking through a veil, and embraced her daughter.

November 20ᵗʰ 1981

Daniel walked briskly along the platform at Penzance and scanned the passengers as they got off the train. It was the final stop so there wasn't the usual harried air of whistles and slamming of doors. There she was. He was no longer shocked at her clothes, although he had been at their first meeting in London two years previously. There she stood in her serge grey habit and wimple.

It had proved harder than he had imagined, tracking her down. Demengel was not a common name. He had managed to trace Milla Demengel up to 1968, where she had been the much-respected Matron at St. Cuthberts, a small cottage hospital in Surrey, after which she seemed to have evaporated into thin air and the trail went cold. He wondered if she had passed away or moved abroad.

At St. Cuthbert's, he had given the number of the hotel he was staying in, to the nurse in charge. She was sorry she could not help this good-looking man with a slight Cornish accent any further. She promised she would ask around the older staff to see if anybody knew what had happened to her. He felt dejected and far from home when he called Dolly that evening.

"I will stay a few more days Dolls. Promise I will do my best."

After more fruitless searching through telephone directories, the phone in his room rang. There was someone in reception to see him. It was the nurse from St. Cuthberts. She slipped him a piece of paper with an address in Godalming. Milla had joined a holy order after having an epiphany of some kind. She was now called Sister Therese, hence the difficulty in tracking her down.

Within days, she was returning to Landscove for the first time since Emmeline's funeral. She told Daniel she had never been told what had happened to Lara. She was astounded to hear that Lara had a baby; even more so that her mother had known and had concealed the truth from them all. It made her suicide more understandable. Milla was full of compassion and guilt for her sister. In latter years, she had tortured herself about the family's abandonment of her. She had long held the view that it was their treatment of her that had precipitated a curse on them all.

There she stood, carrying a small, battered case. "Hello Daniel," she said, offering him a powdery cheek to be kissed.

"Happy Birthday, Milla."

There was a hive of activity back at the beach house.

"Welcome Aunt Milla," Dolly greeted her warmly, relieving her of her case.

"Milla is here Mum," Dolly called. Lara had been in her bedroom, struggling with a zip on her dress. She turned her back so Dolly could fasten it for her.

Milla kissed Lara on the cheek. "Happy Birthday, Lara," she said, aware that this was their first birthday celebration in 60 years.

"Hello book ends," Jack said, kissing his great aunt and grandmother. It made Lara laugh. Milla looked so different in her austere habit, with just her face visible under her headgear. Her face bore the hallmarks of age in a way Lara's did not. She was more lined than Lara and looked every minute of her sixty years whereas Lara looked like a woman in her 40's. None of the usual stressors of life, Shelley had suggested sagely.

Shelley and Vix were due later. They had a special surprise.

"Here he is," Lara said, opening her arms wide for a little boy who ran straight into them. He was dressed in a little shirt and tie and smart dark trousers.

"Enjoy him now, Lara, he won't be looking like that once he gets at that banquet!" laughed Katie, with Dylan bringing up the rear. Katie was pregnant again, in full bloom. She could enjoy a little respite from little Tommy now; he would be glued to Lara's side until they left. It saddened Dolly that Lara had been denied the opportunity to be a mother, although, of course, her life would have been completely different. But Lara was so loving, so funny and Tommy adored her. He loved the funny little song she sang when she rocked him to sleep. She let him make a huge mess in the kitchen as he helped her make tiny cakes and biscuits. He loved looking under the seaweed in the rockpools to find crabs. She was his "Lala". Not a freak, a lunatic, a moral defective or a subnormal. Just his adored Great Grandmother.

In the kitchen, Dolly whispered to Daniel. "No Theo?" She had hoped he would soften his resolve, especially after hearing Milla would be in attendance "No, nothing." Daniel had driven to Chelston Lodge back in 1976. He had had been told by one of the older men in the village who remembered Theo that he was a queer. He had lived with his boyfriend in his mansion since the war. They had denied it, of course, even after homosexuality was decriminalised in 1967. But this was Cornwall, and they were still sodomites as far as the natives were concerned. Chelston Manor had been converted for use as an exclusive hotel in the late '60's, catering for the wealthy elite London crowd. Ask any local, they would tell you it was run by Alex, the fag, and his girlfriend Theo.

Daniel had pushed the service bell in the reception of Chelston Manor. A fat, sweating man had answered the call. A drinker, Daniel correctly assessed. He wore a sweet cologne, expensive, Daniel thought. It barely concealed undertones of gin. He wore a striped blazer and salmon-coloured trousers. He was all smiles and sycophantic politeness; Daniel was extremely handsome, and Theo did so love to feast his eyes on a lithe looking male. Alex was such a bore these days, always complaining about his drinking and calling him a sponger. His mask slipped when Daniel told him the purpose of his visit. As far as he was concerned, Lara had been dead for years. He had no desire to resurrect any contact with her and asked him to leave the hotel. He had been impervious to any overtures to see her. Had Lara known, she would have stopped them; she was not inclined to see him either. She had balked at seeing Milla initially but eventually acceded after much cajoling by Dolly. She only agreed to appease Dolly, although now she was glad she did.

"Come on, Sister Merrigan," Vix teased. Shelley had just been made up to ward sister of Cypress opposite Sister Crisp. They had been regular guests at the Beach house, treated more like friends now than Lara's doctor and nurse.

"How can we hide this big present?" Shelley laughed as they climbed the steps up to the deck. The room had been decorated with balloons and streamers. The long table was groaning under the weight of a veritable feast and a tiered cake, decorated with a large 6 and a 0 in candles.

"Daniel turn the music down, will you," Dolly said, sliding yet another tray of chicken drumsticks from the range.

"Ah, Mum, the girls are here," Dolly said.

Lara kissed Tommy and put him down. She stood up to greet Vix and Shelley. The women stepped apart to reveal the surprise.

"Ta dah!" they said in unison. Between them, grinning broadly, was Mary Ryan.

"Happy birthday, Lara."

The End.

Sian E Jones has recently retired from almost 4 decades of work as a mental health and learning disability nurse. The idea for "The Quiet Room" began to germinate when her parents dropped her off to a hospital for the "mentally subnormal" in 1979 on her eighteenth birthday. She was shocked to discover a cluster of women who had been institutionalised since their adolescence, simply for having an illegitimate child. They had been classified as "moral defectives."

The character of Lara Demengel is based on an amalgam of those women who never got to leave the confines of the hospital. And who bore the punishment, often for the sins of others.

This is her first novel, although she has enjoyed writing short stories for her children and latterly, her Grandchildren.

Now living in her beloved North Wales with her husband, she is a keen outdoor swimmer making the most of her proximity to the sea and the lakes of Snowdonia.

"This book is for all of those survivors who taught me so much". Sian E Jones